THE EN
OUR TETHERS

Alasdair Gray is a fat, spectacled, balding, increasingly old Glasgow pedestrian who (despite two recent years as Professor of Creative Writing at Glasgow University) has mainly lived by writing and designing eighteen books, most of them fiction. THE ENDS OF OUR TETHERS is the ninth published by Canongate.

THE ENDS OF OUR TETHERS

13 Sorry Stories

by

Alasdair Gray

Canongate Books
Edinburgh 2004

First published in 2003 by Canongate Books Ltd,
14 High Street, Edinburgh EH1 1TE

This paperback edition first published in 2004.

10 9 8 7 6 5 4 3 2 1

The publishers gratefully acknowledge a subsidy from the Scottish Arts Council towards the publication of this title.

British Library Cataloguing-in-Publication Data
A catalogue record for this book is available on request from the British Library

ISBN 1 84195 533 7

This paperback edition incorporates the author's final corrections and additions to the first hardback edition.

Typeset by Joe Murray and Forge Design
Printed in Great Britain by
Clays Ltd, St Ives plc

www.canongate.net

FOR AGNES OWENS
One of Our Best

T A B L E   O F

CONTENTS

BIG POCKETS WITH BUTTONED FLAPS

A MILD SEPTEMBER MORNING. A man no longer young strolls thoughtfully on a narrow footpath along a former railway line. Noises tell of a nearby motorway but brambles, elders and hawthorns on each side hide all but the straight empty path ahead until he sees a small clearing among bushes on his right. Two girls sit here at the foot of an old telegraph pole. He pauses, gazing at the top of the cracked grey timber pole. It has cross-pieces with insulators like small white jam pots from which broken wires dangle. He is aware that the girls are in their teens, look surly and

depressed, wear clumsy thick-soled boots and baggy military trousers from which rise pleasantly slim bodies. One says crossly, "What are you staring at?"
"At the wires of that sad sad pole!" says the man without lowering his eyes. "A few years ago they carried messages from this land of ours to a world-wide commercial empire."
"A few years? It was yonks ago," says the girl scornfully. Without looking straight at her the man glimpses a stud piercing her lower lip and one through the wing of a nostril. He says, "Yonks. Yes. I suppose telegraphs were defunct before you were born."
He continues looking up at it until the other girl stands, stretches her arms, pretends to yawn, says, "I'll better away," and walks off through the bushes. Her companion still sits as she did before the stroller arrived.

A minute later he takes a folded newspaper from his coat pocket, unfolds and lays it on the grass where the departed girl was, then sits down with hands folded on the knee of a bent leg. Looking sideways at the girl (who still pretends to ignore him) he says quietly,

"I must ask you a difficult question about . . . about the eff word. Does it shock or annoy you? I don't mean when used as a swear word, I detest swearing, I mean when used as a word for the thing . . . the act lovers do together. Eh?"
After allowing her a moment to reply he speaks briskly as if they had reached an agreement.
"Now I fully realise that a lovely young woman like you —" (she sneers) "— don't sneer, has no wish to eff with a boring old fart like me in bushes beside a derelict railway line. But I suppose you are unemployed and need money?"
"Fucking right I do!" she cries.
"Don't swear. This is an unfair world but I am no hypocrite, I am glad I have money you need. We should therefore discuss how much I am willing to pay for what you are prepared to do. I promise that a wee chat will probably give all the stimulus I need. I have never been greatly enamoured by the down-to-earth, flat-out business of effing."
"Ten pounds!" says the girl, suddenly facing him at last. He nods and says, "Not unreasonable."
"Ten pounds now! Nothing without cash

up front," she says, holding out a hand. From a wallet within his coat he gives her bank notes.
"Thanks," she says, pocketing them and standing up, "Cheerio."
He looks up at her wistfully. She says, "You're too weird for me as well as too old and you're right. This is an unfair world."
She goes off through the bushes. He sighs and sits there, brooding.

Then hears a rustling of leaves. The other girl has returned and stands watching him. He ignores her until she says, "I didnae really go away. I was listening all the time behind that bush."
"Mm."
"I don't think you're weird. Not dangerous-weird. You're just funny."
"Name?" he asks drearily.
"Davida."
"I thought the Scottish custom of making daughters' names out of fathers' names had died out."
"It came back. What's your name?"
"I'm giving nothing else away today Davida. Don't expect it."
But he is looking at her. She grins cheerily

back until he shrugs and pats the grass beside him. She hunkers down slightly further away, hugging her legs with both arms and asking brightly, “What were you going to say to Sharon?”

“You too want cash from me.”

“Aye, some, but not as much as Sharon. Forget about money. Say what you like, I won’t mind.”

He stares at her, opens his mouth, swallows, shuts his eyes very tight and mutters,

“Bigpocketswithbuttonedflaps.”

“Eh?”

“Big,” he explains deliberately. “Pockets. With. Buttoned. Flaps. At last I have said it.”

“They turn you on?” says Davida, looking at her pockets in a puzzled way.

“Yes,” he says defiantly, “because violence is sexy! These pockets are military pockets with room for ammunition clips and grenades and iron rations. On women they look excitingly . . . deliciously . . . unsuitable.”

“Yes, I suppose that’s why they’re in fashion but they’re nothing to get excited about.”

“I enjoy being excited about them,” he groans, covering his face with his hands.

"Were you a school teacher?"
"You'll get nothing more out of me, Davida . . . Why do you think I was a teacher?"
"Because you're bossy as well as polite. Yes, and teachers have to pretend to be better than normal folk so they're bound to go a bit daft when they retire. What did you want with Sharon's pockets that was worth ten quid?"
He looks obstinately away from her.
"Did you want to stick your hands in them like THIS?" she giggles, putting her hands in her pockets. "Did you want to fumble about in them like THIS?"

"No more dirty talk!" orders a very tall thin youth emerging from the bushes, "How dare you molest this young lady with your obscene and suggestive insinuations?"
"ME molest HER? Ha!" cries the man and lies back flat on the grass with hands clasped behind head. He thinks it wise to look as relaxed and unchallenging as possible for he is now greatly outnumbered. Beside the tall youth is a smaller, stouter youth who looks far more menacing because his face is

expressionless, his head completely bald, and beside him stands Sharon saying scornfully, “Big pockets with buttoned flaps!”

“You should have left us alone a bit longer,” grumbles Davida. “He was starting to enjoy himself.”

“He was starting to enjoy his antisocial fetishistic propensities with a lassie young enough to be his grand-daughter!” cries the tall youth fiercely.

“Molesting two lassies in fifteen minutes!” says Sharon. “We’ve witnesses to prove it. He’s got to pay us for that.”

The man says, “I’ve paid you already.”

“That . . . is not an attitude . . . I would advocate if you want to stay in one piece,” says the tall boy slowly taking from a big pocket in his trousers a knife with a long blade. The smaller, more dangerous-looking youth says, “Hullo, Mr McCorquodale.”

The man sits up to see him better and asks, “How’s the family, Shon?”

“Dad isnae out yet,” says the shorter boy, “but Sheila’s doing well in TV rentals. She went to Australia.”

“Yes Sheila was the smartest of you. I

advised her to emigrate."

"I KNEW he was a teacher," says Davida smugly.

"You stupid fucking cretin!" the tall boy yells at the shorter one, "If you'd kept out the way we could have rolled him for all he's got, buggered off and nothing would have happened! We don't live round here, we've no police record, nobody could have found us! But now he knows you we'll have to evade identification by cutting off his head and hands and burying them miles away!"

He saws the air wildly with the knife. The girls' faces express disgust. The smaller youth says mildly, "Don't do that to old Corky, he wasnae one of the worst."

"Not one of the worst?" cries the ex-teacher jumping to his feet with surprising agility, "Did I not make my gym a living hell for you and your brothers? I also advise YOU," he tells the taller youth, "to put that knife away. You obviously don't know how to handle it."

"And you do?" says the tall boy sarcastically.

"Yes, son, I do. I served five years in the army before I took to teaching. Your combat training is all from television and video games. I have learned armed AND unarmed combat from professional killers paid by the British government. Davida. Sharon. Shon. Persuade your friend to pocket that bread knife. Tell him he's a fine big fellow but I'm stronger than I look and if he's really interested in dirty fighting I can show him some tricks that'll have the eyes popping out of his head. Tell him I gave Sharon nearly all the money I carry so if he needs more he'll have to come home with me."

And McCorquodale smiles rather
wistfully at the tall youth's
combat trousers.

SWAN BURIAL

I PHONE OUR ADMINISTRATOR and say that in ten minutes I will bring her the overdue assessments. She says, "Thank you, Doctor Gowry. And will you also bring the introduction to the new handbook?"

"That will take a little longer, Karen, perhaps another hour."

"Then don't bother bringing me all these things today. Leave the assessed portfolios and introduction in my front-office pigeon hole when you go home tonight. I'll process them first thing tomorrow."

"Thank you Karen, that would be much more convenient."

"I'm *Phyllis*, Doctor Gowry. Karen left three months ago."

"Haha, so she did. Sorry, Phyllis."

I finish assessing the portfolios on my desk, look for the others and remember I took them home three days ago. Never mind. I'll rise early tomorrow and bring them to the front office before Karen arrives. So now I tackle the introduction, though I fear this job is getting beyond me and I should apply for something less demanding. Which reminds me that I *have* applied for another job, with Human Resources, and must soon attend an interview for it. But first, the introduction. This should be easy. I need only bring the introduction to last year's handbook up to date by changing a word here or there.

But revising the old introduction turns out to be almost impossible. I wrote it only a year ago but the language now strikes me as long-winded official jargon, misleading when not practically meaningless. It was written to attract folk with money into an organisation I now want to leave, but surely that can be done in a few simple, honest sentences? I try and try to write them and have almost glimpsed how to do it when I see the the time is nearly four P.M! My interview with Human Resources is at four fifteen! If I run to the main road and catch a taxi at once I can still be in time so *run*.

Rain is falling, every passing taxi is engaged, at ten past four I decide to phone Human Resources, apologise, blame the weather and if possible postpone the interview. I rush into a familiar pub and find the public telephone has been replaced by a flashing machine that gives the users an illusion of shooting people. I groan. A man I know asks why. I say, “No telephone.”
“Use my mobile,” he says, holding out what looks like a double nine domino.
“Thank you – thank you – but I don’t know how to use such a machine.”
“I’ll dial for you. What number?”
I cannot tell him, for the number is in a diary on my office desk. He offers to dial directory enquiries but, suddenly full of black certainty that I have now no chance of the Human Resources job, instead I order a large whisky for each of us.

He says, “Thanks. Cheers. You seem troubled. Tell me your woes.”
I do so in great detail, during which he buys us each another drink. At last he says, “Remarkable. Remarkable. But why apply

to Human Resources? It doesn't even figure in the Dow Jones index. You're a metallurgist so you should apply to Domestic Steel. It died in the late sixties but a renaissance is due and your age and experience would make you a valuable link with the past."

I ponder these words and find that they also strike me as meaningless official jargon. I order another round of drinks and tell him I mainly regret losing my chance with Human Resources because of my wife. She feels my job with Scottish Arterial is killing me. The man says, "I suspect you need a total change of scene. Any plans for a holiday this year?"

I say, "Not this year," and explain that my wife hates leaving home, even for a few days, because she is sure we cannot afford it. She says such suggestions threaten our marriage and make her feel I am battering her. I then notice it is twenty minutes to ten, say goodbye and leave, but as usual nowadays I call for a quick drink at two or three other pubs on my way home.

I open our front door shortly after midnight and hear gentle snoring from the darkened bedroom. I undress without switching on the light but the window curtains are not completely drawn. By gleams from a street lamp outside I see a tumbler of clear liquid on my wife's bedside table. Is it water? Gin? Vodka? Does she drink as much alcohol in my absence as I do in hers? I refrain from investigating and slip in beside her. The rhythm of her snores alters slightly as she snuggles cosily against me. I lie basking in that cosiness. This is now the pleasantest part of my life; perhaps it always was. She mutters something that sounds like "I wish she had chosen a different star."

"Who are you talking about?" I ask. She is obviously talking in her sleep, but even then can sometimes answer questions. After a moment she mutters that they're burying the bird.

"What bird?" I ask, trying to imagine the dream she is having. After a while she says, "A swan."

Her dreams are as impenetrable as my own.

I continue basking in her warmth, dimly haunted by a feeling that tomorrow I should rise early and do something. I cannot remember what, but Karen will know. Karen is amazingly efficient and good at covering up for me; besides, nowadays in Britain no professional person as close to retiral as I am is ever sacked for inefficiency.

I wait patiently for sleep
to cover me all up
like a cloak.

NO BLUEBEARD

BEFORE TALKING ABOUT Tilda I'll mention earlier wives. Wife 1 was an ordinary tidy home-lover. We met at secondary school and after leaving it she let us make love then refused to allow any more of that unless we married. So we married. Wife 2 was a bossy manager, wife 3 very quiet and messy. I married all of them because it made us feel more secure for a while and separated from them without fuss or fighting, so I am obviously no Bluebeard. Indeed, most of my life has passed in sexual loneliness which makes me hopeful when a new affair looks like starting, as happened a year ago.

In the park near my home I saw a couple stand quarrelling under a tree. No one else was in sight but they were yards away from me and I expected to pass without being noticed. Instead the woman rushed over to me saying, "Please help me, sir, that man is frightening me."

"Good riddance!" shouted the man and hurried away leaving us facing each other.

She was in her late teens or early twenties, big and beautiful in a plain undecorated way, with short brown hair and a determined expression that showed she was no victim. Victims don't attract me. Her clothes were of very good quality and conventional in a smart country-wear style, yet seemed slightly odd, either because they did not perfectly match or were more suited to an older woman. The silence between us grew embarrassing. I asked if she would like a coffee. She seized my hand saying, "Lead the way," and I found us walking toward a hotel outside the park gates, gates through which the man who had shouted at us was rapidly vanishing without a backward glance. We walked side by side so easily that I thought she was leading me, though later I found she knew nothing of the neighbourhood. I asked her name. She said, "Mattie or

Tilda, take your pick."
"Surname?"
"*That*," she said emphatically, "is what they want me not to advertise. The less said about *that* the better you cunt."
Her loud clear voice had the posh accent that strikes most Scottish ears as English. I decided she was an eccentric aristocrat and suddenly, because I am a conventional soul, had no wish to take her to a hotel lounge or anywhere public. I suggested going to my place. She said, "Lead on," so I did.

We had not far to go and as we swung along she murmured, "Cunt cunt. Cunt cunt," very quietly to herself as if hoping no one heard. That excited me. My flat is a large bed-sitting room, workroom, bathroom and kitchen. She stood in the largest room and announced, "This is certainly more salubrious than that other man's place."
As I helped to remove her coat she whispered, "You cunt," which I took as an invitation to help her out of more garments. She muttered, "Right, carry on."
I led her to the bed. What followed was so simple and satisfying that afterwards I lay

completely relaxed for the first time in years, almost unable to believe my good luck.
"And now," she said, lying flat on her back and talking loudly as if to the ceiling, "I want apple tart with lots and lots of cream on top. *Ice* cream."
"Your wish is my command," I said jumping up and dressing.

The nearest provision store was a street away. I returned in less than fifteen minutes and found her in the middle of the floor, clutching her hair and dressed as if her clothes had been thrust on in panic. She screamed, "*Where have you been?*"
"Buying what you ordered," I said, displaying tart and ice cream. She slumped grumpily into a chair while I prepared them in the kitchen. Later, while eating, I asked what had made her hysterical. She said, "You left me alone in this strange house and I thought you would come back hours later stinking of whisky and wanting us to do it again."
I did want us to do it again but was not greedy enough to insist. I told her I was a freelance programmer who worked at home and I detested booze because my

dad had been alcoholic. She looked pleased then said slowly and slyly, "Regarding the dad situation, ditto. Ditto but if disorder is confined to the family apartments others do not notice. And if you too detest alcohol and work at home like all sensible people it is possible, cunt, that you may be possible."

I laughed at that and said, "Possibly you are too. Where are you from?"

"I have already said they do not want me to say."

I explained that I was not interested in her disgustingly snobbish family but assumed she had not been long in Glasgow. She said cautiously, "Until the day before yesterday, or maybe the day before that, I occupied a quite nice caravan in a field of them. People came and went. Mostly went."

"There must have been a town or village near your caravan park."

"There was a village and the sea but neither was convenient. I ate in a hotel called The Red Fox. I met the man who brought me here in The Red Fox. He turned out to be most unpleasant, not my sort at all."

"Have you things in his house? Things you want to collect?"

"What things?"
"A nightgown? Clothes?"
"No. Certainly not. Not at all. Please don't be a . . . " She hesitated then said quickly, "cunt give me a glass of milk."
It is almost impossible to judge the intelligence of someone from an alien culture so I have never discovered exactly how stupid or mad Tilda is. She behaved as if she expected to live with me. I wanted that too so it was hardly a sign of *her* insanity. Lunatics are supposed to have delusions. Tilda had none. She said what she meant or expected in a few clear words that always made sense. Only secrecy about her family and her compulsion to say cunt were inexplicable at first, and from remarks she passed in the following two weeks I soon pieced together an explanation.

Her "people" (she never said father or mother) ran a residential hotel or nursing home for "people of our own sort". They seemed a pernickety sort because "everything has to be just so."
I asked what just so meant. She said, "Exactly right forever and ever world without end amen. Dinner was awful. We

had to dress."

"In tuxedos and black ties?"

"Tuxedo is an American word. We British say evening dress. Female evening wear is less uniform than male attire but more taxing. Little hankies are an endless ordeal. I fidgeted with mine which is *not the done thing*, in fact *utterly wrong*, in fact *a rotten way to carry on* and I became quite impossible when I started (cunt) using (cunt) that word (cunt cunt)."

Tilda's use of that word had obviously been an unconscious but sensible device to escape from bullying relations. They had lodged her in a caravan park very far from them ("half a day's car ride away") and made her promise not to mention their name because "if word gets around it will be bad for the business and we aren't exactly rolling in money."

This made me think their business was a sanatorium for rich mental defectives whose guardians might have doubts about the establishment if they knew people on the staff had an eccentric daughter. I suspected too that Tilda's people were less posh than they wished. The few very posh people I have met care nothing for elaborate etiquette and swear like labourers.

But Tilda's family had given her worse eccentricities than that Anglo-Saxon word.

Next day I arose later than usual, made breakfast, gave Tilda hers on a tray in bed and got down to business. At ten she came into the workroom wearing my dressing gown and sat on the floor with her back to the wall, placidly watching figures and images I manipulated on the screen. Shortly after eleven she announced that she wanted a coffee. I said, "Good idea. Make me one too."

She cried indignantly, "I can't do that! I don't know how!"

"I'll tell you how," I said, treating the matter as a joke, "In the kitchen you will see an electric kettle on a board by the sink. Fill it with tap water and switch on the heat. There is also a jar of instant coffee powder on the board, a drawer of cutlery below, mugs hanging on hooks above. Take two mugs, put a small spoonful of powder in each, add boiling water and stir. Add milk and sugar to yours if you like, but I take my coffee black."

She stamped out of the room and shortly returned with a mug she slammed down defiantly on my worktop. It contained lukewarm water with brown grains floating on top. When I complained she said, "I *told* you I can't make coffee."

I found that Tilda could wash and dress herself, eat and drink politely, talk clearly and truthfully and also (though I didn't know how she learned it) fuck with astonishing ease. Everything else had been done for her so she stubbornly refused to learn anything else.

Despite which our first weeks together were very happy. She added little to my housework. Former wives had insisted on making meals or being taken out for them. Tilda ate what I served without a word of complaint, nor did she litter the rooms with cosmetic tubes, powders, lotions, toilet tissues, fashion magazines and bags of shopping. She hated shopping and refused to handle money. I gathered that "her people" had never given her any, paying the caravan rent and Red Fox food bills by bank order. She brought to my house only the clothes she wore, clothes passed to her by someone of similar size, I think an older sister. By threatening to chuck her out unless she accompanied me and by ordering a taxi I got her into the women's department of Marks and Spencer. Buying her clothes was not the slightly erotic adventure I had hoped as she cared nothing for what she wore and would have let me dress her like an outrageous prostitute had the garments been comfortable. But there is no fun in buying sexy clothes for folk who don't feel sexy, so I bought simple, conventional garments of the kind her sister had given, but more modern and in better-matching colours. I did not then notice that her attitude to clothes and making love were the same. She never restricted the pleasures I had with her in bed once or twice a night, so only later did I see she was indifferent to them.

Being together outside bed was also easy because we had no social life and did not want one. Since expulsion from her people's "rather grand place" her only society seemed to have been fellow diners in The Red Fox, and she would not have eloped with "that other man" if she had liked them much. My own social life once depended on friends met through my wives and a job in local housing, but during the last marriage I had become a freelance working at home, which perhaps drove away wife number 3. Since then I had managed without friends, parties *et cetera*. I like films and jazz I enjoyed in my teens. I play them on my computer and discuss them over the internet with fellow enthusiasts in England, Denmark and America so need no other society. An afternoon stroll in the park kept me fit. Tilda managed without even that. Apart from the Marks and Spencer's visit she has only left the flat once since entering it.

Our daily routine was this. After an early morning cuddle I rose, made breakfast, gave Tilda hers in bed, laid out her clothes for the day, put dirty clothes in the washing machine, started work. Tilda arose around ten, I made coffee for us at eleven thirty and a snack lunch at one. Then came my afternoon stroll and shopping expedition which she bitterly resented. I insisted on being away for at least ninety minutes but had to mark the exact minute of return on the clock face, and if I was a single minute late she got into a furious sulk. Then came a cup of tea and biscuit, then two or three hours of more programming, then I made the evening meal, we consumed it, I did some housework, internetted for a little and so to bed. And wherever I was working Tilda sat on the floor, looking perfectly relaxed, sometimes frowning and pouting but often with a strange little satisfied smile. I assumed she was remembering the people and place she had escaped from. I once asked what she was thinking about and she murmured absent-mindedly, "Least said soonest mended. Curiosity killed the cat."

I asked if she would like a television set? A Walkman radio? Magazines? She said, "A properly furnished mind cunt is its own feast cunt and does not need such expensive and foolish extravagancies."

But she did not often use the cunt word now and when she saw an arresting image on my screen sometimes asked about it. I always answered fully and without technical jargon. Sometimes she heard me out and said "Right", sometimes cut me short with a crisp "Enough said", so I never knew how much she understood. When someone speaks with the accent and idiom of British cabinet ministers and bank managers and company directors it is hard not to suspect them of intelligence. I sometimes think even now that Tilda might be trained to use a computer. Many undeveloped minds take to it easily, having nothing to unlearn.

But during our mid-day snack one day the entry-phone rang very loud and long. Tilda stared at me in alarm.

"A parcel delivery," I said to reassure her, but without believing it. Part of me had been expecting such a ring. A crisp voice on the phone said, "I am here to see Matilda and if you try to stop me I will summon the police."

I opened the door to a tiny old woman who looked nothing like Tilda except for the determined look on her terribly lined face.

"You are?" I asked, thinking she was a grandmother or aunt. She walked past me into the lobby saying, "Where?"

I pointed to the sitting-room doorway and followed her through.

Tilda sat at the end of a sofa where I had left her but her arms were now folded tightly round her body and she had turned to face the wall.

"Well!" said the little woman. Standing

in the middle of the floor she drew a deep breath and thus addressed the back of Tilda's head.

"You will be *pleased* to hear, *delighted* to know, *ecstatic* to be informed that it has cost us a very pretty penny in private detectives to track you here. A small fortune. More than a family not exactly rolling in wealth can afford, you *ungrateful*, *inconsiderate*, *selfish*, *shameless*, *debauched* what? What shall I call you? Slut is too mild a word but I refuse to soil my lips with anything more accurate. And you, sir!" – she turned to me – "You cannot alas be sued for abducting a minor but we have lawyers who will make you wish you had never been born if you try to get as much as a farthing out of us. Not a chance. No dice. *Nothing doing sonny boy.*"

I told her I had no intention of getting money out of Tilda or her family. She said, "Fine words butter no parsnips. Are you going to marry her?"

I said we had not yet discussed that. She told the back of Tilda's head, "Make him marry you. It's your one chance of security." She then strolled round my flat as if she was the only one in it, fingering curtains and furnishings and examining ornaments while I stared in amazement. Returning from an inspection of workroom, kitchen and lavatory she spoke as firmly but less fiercely.

"Matilda, I admit this is not the Glasgow hell-hole the detective agency led me to expect. Maybe you have landed lucky. This second cavalier of yours certainly seems more presentable than what I have heard about the first who picked you up. So marry this one. *We* don't want you. Having made that crystal clear I will take my leave. I have a car waiting. Goodbye."

"Come back!" I cried as she turned to go, for I was angry and wished to annoy her, "Come back! Your address please."

"What can *you* possibly want with *my* address?"

I told her I was willing to believe Tilda had been brought up so meanly that she had no personal belongings in what was once her home, but marriage had been mentioned. That would need copies of a birth certificate and notification of her parents' occupations and place of residence. The little old lady said, "Oh, very haughty. Very cunning."

She took a printed card from a purse, laid

it on a sideboard and, scribbling on it with a slim small pencil, said through clenched teeth, "I am substituting – my name – for your father's, Matilda, because he died a fortnight ago of a stroke in his bath. Not a messy business thank goodness. This news *of course* holds no interest for you. All the affection was on *his* side, though it was not a very exalted form of affection and you might have done more to discourage him. I can leave now, I think."

She had been perhaps ten minutes in the flat but it now felt as if she had burned huge dirty holes with a flame-thrower in floor, walls and ceiling. I wanted to go outside and walk in the fresh air, but could not persuade Tilda to move or turn her face from the wall. I tried soothing words but she stayed silent. I laid my hand gently on her shoulder but she shook it off and sat where she was until long after nightfall. When she came to bed at last she would not let me cuddle her but lay as far from me as possible. Next day she did not get up and hardly touched the food I brought. I could not bear to leave her alone in the house that afternoon. At night when I came to bed I discovered she had peed in it. That made me furious enough to drag her out and wash her. While making a clean bed on the floor I told her I would send for a doctor if she did not pull herself together. She said nothing. I asked if she wanted me to send for a doctor. She said, "If you do I will scream."

I told her that if she screamed when a doctor came he would quickly whisk her into a mental hospital. At this she turned her face to the wall again.

"Tilda," I said, pleading, "I realise your father's death has been a terrible shock, but you mustn't just lie down and fall apart. Is there nothing I can do to help?"

She muttered, "You *know* what you can do."

"Honestly, Tilda, I don't know! How can I know?"

"Because she told you."

"Who told me?"

"My mother told you. Twice."

That our wicked little visitor was Tilda's mother had never occurred to me. I thought furiously back over her words then said, "If you mean, Tilda, that you want us to marry, of course I'll do it if that will restore us to being as friendly and loving as we were before *she* stormed in."

"Don't bank on it!" said Tilda bitterly between clenched teeth, sounding so like her mother that I felt the short hairs on my neck bristle. I tried to be reasonable and explained there was no point in marrying if it did us no good. She neither answered nor turned her head but I saw tears pouring from her eyes, saw she was shuddering with soundless sobs. What horrible training had taught her to weep noiselessly? The sight maddened me. The madness took the form of promising to marry her as soon as possible. At last I got her into the clean new improvised bed and we fell asleep cuddling again. Something had been regained and something lost. Tilda's mother had brought me to the same start as my previous marriages.

Several days had to elapse before the marriage. During them Tilda refused me the lovemaking I had once taken for granted, but we cuddled at night and steady cuddling has always nourished me more than the irregular pleasures of fucking. I was also fool enough to think that, despite the past, we had a honeymoon ahead and suggested visiting

Spain, Greece or Barbados.

"Why?" asked Tilda.

I pointed to colourful pictures in a spread of travel brochures and said, "Bright sunshine. Blue skies. Warm sea. Soft sand."

"Foolish extravagance and a waste of good money. We aren't exactly rolling in it."

"The money is mine, Tilda, and I promise I have enough to easily pay for a trip."

"Nobody who knows anything about money *ever* has enough," she said contemptuously. I was glad she no longer seemed pathetic. Nowadays on rising she sat around the sitting room instead of joining me in the workroom. It was a healthy sign of growing independence, though I missed her silent company.

I wrote to tell Tilda's mother of the wedding, suggested one of her family should witness it, received in reply a card saying, "My brother-in-law will attend." We met him at the registry office: a big laconic man with an expression suggesting all that happened was his own very private little joke. I suspected him of being a highly self-controlled drunkard though he smelled of nothing worse than the tweeds he wore. The witness I had invited was

Henderson, a freelance programmer whose character was like mine – we shared business when one of us had too much of it. After the signing I took the four of us for a meal at The Ubiquitous Chip despite Tilda muttering, "Do we have to do this?" She refused to drink anything but soda water and lime or eat anything but ice cream. For us men her uncle ordered pre-prandial brandies, wine with the food, and after the dessert an astonishingly expensive champagne with which he gave a toast prefaced by the words, "Be upstanding." He and I and Henderson stood holding fluted glasses with what resembled mist arising from them while Tilda sat glowering into her third dish of ice cream. Her uncle said, "Here's to the blushing bride. Here's also, more importantly I think, to a very honourable groom. You!" – he suddenly stared straight at me without the faintest trace of a smile – "You are a better man than I am, Gunga Din." He emptied his glass, said he must rush for a train and left. I am unable to regard him as a parasitic clown because later I found he had paid for the drink, which cost much more than the food.

Tilda and I went home, both entering the flat with sighs of obvious relief. Tenderly I helped her off with her outer garments and was about to undo inner ones when she said, "Don't be silly."

I shrugged and we sat facing each other across the hearth rug. Then she said slowly and firmly, "I *think*. It is *time*. I had a bed *of my own*."

I gaped at her for at least a minute before asking why. She said, "Why not? My mother and father sleep, no, *slept* you cunt in different beds, in fact different bedrooms. The best people do."

That thrust me into a confusion of thoughts and feelings from which the most definite to surface was the most mean and trivial: I regretted having thrown out the old mattress and getting another, because if she insisted on sleeping alone she could have done it on the bedding she had wet. And she did insist on sleeping alone. I argued with her of course, at one point was on the verge of threatening violence when tears started from her eyes and I knew unbearable silent sobbing would begin if I persisted. I made a bed for myself on the sofa then decided to go for a walk and brood over this new, alarming development, but she screamed, "You can't leave me alone here *now*!" And I couldn't. I saw that without me Tilda would melt down into nothing but helpless, terrible misery. I was trapped and could only break out of the trap by acting like a beast. I could not call a doctor and tell him that the woman I had married that afternoon was now certifiably insane.

I made myself a bed on the sofa. Without Tilda's body to snuggle against I was unable to sleep but found the situation oddly familiar. She was now rejecting me like three previous wives who began by liking me then found they could not. I had blamed neither them nor myself for that – a calm, uncomprehending acceptance had seemed the sanest attitude. It now felt like madness to try seeing why everyone I loved had rejected me, but I had nothing else to do. The simplest explanation was the old Freudian one that, like most men, I married women who resembled my mother, thus condemning myself to enact the same stupid drama with each. But my mother had been nervous and clinging, a type I avoid. Apart from strong wills and their wish to marry me wives 1, 2 and 3 had been as different from each other as they were from wife 4.

Number 1 had this in common with my mother: she expected and wanted to be a housewife. Before the 1960s most wives outside the poorly paid classes expected to be supported at home, because they were fully employed there. Before washing machines, good housewives scrubbed and wrung clothes for body and bed by hand – ironed and mended them – knitted socks and other woollen items – cut, sewed, embroidered garments, curtains, cushions and chair covers. Before vacuum cleaners they drove dust out of carpets by hanging them outdoors and whacking them with canes. Shopping was more frequent before refrigerators and freezers because foods had to be eaten near the time of purchase. Good wives baked scones, biscuits, cakes, tarts, puddings, made jams, jellies, pickles and an exquisite sweet called *tablet*, for which everyone had a slightly different recipe. They regularly cleaned and polished linoleum, glass, metal and wooden surfaces. Their homes were continually restored works of art, exhibited once a week at a small afternoon tea party for friends and neighbours who were similar wives.

Number 1 had looked forward to that life, though we acquired every sensible labour-saving appliance available in 1972 having saved up for them through a three-year engagement when we lived with our parents. She gave up her teaching job just before the wedding after making sure all our well-wishers would give us useful presents. We had a short honeymoon in Rothesay then moved to a rented flat in Knightswood, the earliest and, in the year 2002, still poshest of Glasgow's housing schemes. We were very happy at first. The washing machine, Hoover *et cetera* left her free to whitewash ceilings, re-paper walls and carry out many improvements I thought unnecessary, as previous tenants had left the flat in excellent condition. My job in a local housing department office let me walk home for lunch. On Friday nights we went to a film or theatre, at weekends had polite little dinner or bridge parties with other couples, and on most evenings found entertainment in television and a game of cribbage before the small snack we called supper. And so to bed.

I was pulling on a condom after undressing one evening when she suggested we should have a child. It had not occurred to me that her domestic activity was a form of nest-building. Perhaps because I was my parents' only child I dislike children, so suggested we wait a bit before starting to multiply ourselves: we should first get a bigger house, a bungalow in King's Park or Bearsden, which would be possible when I was promoted to head office and able to pay a large deposit for a mortgage. She said grimly, "If it's a matter of *payment* I'll go back to teaching and earn us more money that way. But you'll have to take your share of housework. I can't bring in a wage *and* do everything else."

I said I did not want her to go back to teaching; we were still young and had no need for impatience. She did not reply but refused to make love that night and (though my memory may be at fault – this was nearly thirty years ago) I think we never made love again. She returned to teaching, I started doing the shopping and would have made meals too, but she refused them. When I suggested that I could make meals as good as those my mother made she said, "That's why I'd find them inedible."

A month or two later I remarked that only a third of her weekly wage was being deposited in our joint bank account. She said, "That's because I do at least two thirds of our housework. You may think you do half but you don't."

I shrugged and said, "So be it."

She began going out once or twice a week with teacher friends. My promotion to head office came sooner than I expected. I began lunching in a snack bar with a colleague who also enjoyed cribbage and had a folding board we played upon. His system of marking was different from mine and more interesting. I explained it to my wife one evening while dealing the cards. She flung hers down saying, "If you're going to change the rules of this bloody awful game I'm done with it."

I realised that for months she had been pleasing me by playing a game she detested and suddenly I felt for her a terrible loving pity. Had she told the truth at the start I could easily have done without cribbage because we had enjoyed so many other things together – meals and films and small polite parties and lovemaking. But maybe she had only pretended to enjoy these things too because she loved, not me, but a conventional marriage.

One evening she explained she was having a steady love affair with a colleague and wanted to divorce me. I took several minutes to absorb the shock of this.

"If," I said carefully, "you really need a child let us make one. Let us make it now. We don't need someone else to give you one of *those.*"

She smiled mournfully and said, "Too late, you poor old soul."

I was only twenty-four but shrugged and said again, "So be it." In those days divorce by mutual consent was impossible under Scots law; one of the parties had to get it by proving the other's misconduct. She gave me proof of her misconduct, I passed it to a lawyer and paid for half the costs of the action. I moved to a boarding-house leaving her the flat with all its furnishings so she had no reason for a grudge against me.

Years later at an office party I danced with a very lively little stranger. She had huge eyes, a mass of thick black hair, a slightly transatlantic accent and told me she was Polish-Canadian. Contact with her was so exciting that I asked her back to my place. She rolled the pupils of her eyes upwards and murmured, "No, no, impossible tonight, Charlie is very jealous. But we will keep in touch."

We did. I learned that both Charlie and her husband worked for the housing department. One morning the husband stopped me as we passed in a corridor and said, "You know my wife, I think. Has she told you I am divorcing her for promiscuity?"

She had told me but I denied it. He said, "Yes. For promiscuity. Don't worry, you will not be cited in court, you are only her latest. Steer clear of her if you value your sanity."

I thanked him for the advice but was enjoying my casual affair too much to take it. That she had Charlie as well as me made it all the more casual.

One Sunday afternoon she arrived unexpectedly at my lodgings in a state of happy excitement. Early that morning she had discussed Charlie with a close woman friend who had burst into tears and confessed that she too was having an affair with Charlie.

"Guess what I did then?" cried number 2. "I calmed her and cheered her up then rushed round to Charlie's place and said, 'Sit down, I've news for you.' He went as white as a sheet. I told him I knew he'd been having it off with Sharon but I didn't mind at all because I've been having it off with you. So now we can all carry on with our new partners and everything will be fine! Isn't that wonderful? Now you can come and live with me!"

Though foreseeing she would almost certainly marry me I pretended to agree that this was wonderful.

Her home was beside the Botanic Gardens. She had her office there and was the first in Glasgow – perhaps in Scotland – to run a dating and escort business by computer and telephone. It was a profitable business. She ran it efficiently yet insisted on also doing everything good Scottish housewives did, refusing all assistance because she was sure only she could do such things properly. Luckily she wanted no more children, having two girls and a son in their teens who often visited her but preferred their father's house because, she said, "They think I'm too much of a bossy-boots."

She was certainly bossy. She both gave and was asked to many parties, and before setting out would glare at something I wore and say, "I refuse to be seen with you wearing that!"

"What's wrong with it?"

"It's years out of date. Ten or twenty years out of date."

"Male clothing doesn't date like women's does."

"That shows you know nothing about it."

Yet she was generous and I had no objection to the new clothes she bought me: they always fitted well and were smart without being eccentric. But I was appalled when I came home one evening and found she had given all my former clothes to Oxfam, so appalled that I packed the few things I needed with the firm intention of leaving that house forever, though invitations had been posted for our wedding reception a fortnight hence. She had a master key and used it to lock me in. I managed to open a window and would have jumped out but her anger suddenly turned to a terrible storm of weeping and pleading. I had never before seen anyone in that state. I could not possibly leave her in it, so stayed and comforted her until we were friends again and got married after all.

Through number 2 I met people whose lives seemed jumpier and more erratic than I was used to: journalists, broadcasters, women who managed their own shops. All had children by former husbands or wives and lived with partners they seemed to leave or change without conspicuous fuss. Despite her ex-husband's warning I am sure number 2 was not promiscuous while we lived together. She enjoyed declaring her feelings too openly to hide them for long and in five or six years confessed only twice to having brief affairs with other men. These confessions were made partly to annoy me so I annoyed her back by saying I did not care what she did when I could not see it, which was true. Yet despite our main faithfulness to each other, and the lovely tricks and eccentricities by which she turned ordinary meals and events into pleasant occasions, every month came a huge explosion of grief and rage which made a hell of that marriage. They were provoked by trivialities that I could never foresee and can now hardly remember. I think her love of drama was the main cause. While stooping to lift a fallen pencil at work I struck the corner of a desk with my brow and raised a small lump. When I got home she screamed, "What's happened to your face? You look horrible!"

I could not take that seriously and a week later referred to it as proof of how easily she was upset. She laughed and said, "I wasn't upset at all! I just felt wicked and wanted to annoy you."

But the longer we lived together the more explosive our quarrels became until I was pointing out, again and again, that the misery we gave each other was far greater than the comfort. But whenever I packed up to leave, again and again came appalling grief of the sort that had got me marrying her after seeing it was a bad idea.

She was fond of children, the younger

the better, and was visiting someone with a new baby one evening when I decided to eat out alone. In the restaurant I met friends of number 2 with a woman I had never seen before. They invited me to join them, jocularly remarking that this was the first time they had ever seen me without a wife. I enjoyed that meal, drank more than my usual glass of wine and found the friends were leaving me with the stranger. "Don't worry, we won't clype," they said, pretending to creep away on tiptoe. So I spent that night in the stranger's home.

I call my wives by number instead of name to shield them from readers who may meet them, and I also disguise them with a few inaccuracies. With this in mind let me say that number 3 was a senior hospital nurse of a sort that used to be called matrons. She was as tall as me but so slimly built that she looked taller, with a delicate oval head and a thatch of blonde hair cut very short. More attractive than her beauty was her quietness. When not sleeping or sulking number 2 talked almost incessantly, often with questions that needed highly detailed answers. Number 3 used few words, never gossiped and seldom asked questions. Being unused to long silences I found hers disconcerting at first and tried to fill them with entertaining chatter but she murmured, "You don't *need* to talk to me."

Before I left next morning we had come to one of the unexpected understandings that have changed my life.

"I want to live with you," I told her. "I am going straight home to tell my wife that. Have you room for me?"

"That depends on how much you bring with you," she said with a Mona Lisa smile.

She lived south of the river, not far from Queen's Park. Returning by bus I had plenty of time to plan what to tell number 2 and to imagine the hideous emotional explosion it would cause. My courage completely failed. I saw I hadn't the guts to be so cruel and ended by inventing a lie to explain my overnight absence. I found 2 moodily working at her computer. She did not look up or turn round when I explained to her truthfully how, the previous night, I had met the friends who said they would not clype on me, adding only that I had gone home with them for a nightcap and fallen asleep. But she knew the addition was untrue because very early that morning she had phoned them while phoning everybody else she knew in search of me. She asked if I had spent the night with a woman.

"Yes, but nobody you know," I said. The result was less violent than I had feared. She switched off the machine, bowed her face into her hands and in a muffled voice said she could do no more work that day, though it was Saturday, usually her busiest day. She behaved, and I acted, as if she was suffering from something like the death of a parent, something that left her too numb for outrage. I took her for a walk through the Botanic Gardens and up Kelvindale to the canal towpath. It was a mild, very pleasant spring day. We exchanged a few words about unimportant things, dined in a pub near Anniesland Cross and were returning home before she said, "Do you want to leave me for this woman I don't know?"

"Yes," I said.

"If you had said no," she told me mournfully, "and begged and wept and pleaded like I sometimes do we could have gone on living together. But now I can't

help seeing that you really don't want me, so it's goodbye."
She then wept a little, but very quietly, and that was the end of that because divorce by mutual consent was now as easy in Scotland as in England.

Number 3's home (where I still live) was the basement and former kitchen quarters of a large Victorian terrace house divided into flats. The front windows looked into a sunken area and a back door opened on to a long narrow garden, a garden number 3 looked after beautifully for she preferred gardening to housework. I never knew a woman who seemed to care less for her home.

It was sparsely furnished with few of the ornaments and knick-knacks most women accumulate. She had lived there fifteen years, long enough to pay off her mortgage on it, but wallpaper and linoleum had obviously been inherited from earlier tenants, while a cumbersome gas cooker and huge earthenware sink with brass taps seemed as old as the building. I wanted to pay for having the kitchen completely modernised but she said firmly, "No, I'll pay for that. I promised myself a new kitchen ages ago and I know someone who will do the job cheaply."

I refrained from saying that all jobs done cheaply are done badly. Instead I offered to put in double-glazed windows and have the whole place re-painted, re-papered and carpeted. She agreed to this and let me choose colours and patterns because she wasn't interested in these things. I was intensely interested because I had decided, with her permission, to make this flat the headquarters of a new business. I was tired of working for the housing department.

When I joined it in the early seventies Glasgow was still a partly socialist city state owning its own lighting, transport, water and schooling. It was the largest landlord of public housing outside London and proud of the fact, because John Wheatley, a Glasgow politician, had passed the act that made local government housing possible. By the 1980s central government pressure to privatise public property seemed irresistible, and Glasgow's ruling Labour party put up no resistance at all. Soon after it became legal for council tenants to buy their houses the council appointed a housing chief who publicly announced that Glasgow city council was the biggest owner of slum property in Britain. We in his department looked forward with great interest to his remedy. After a few months he resigned the post and started an agency helping private housing companies to buy local government property. Having had access to municipal housing records he knew, of course, the properties people with money would most want to buy. This would once have been thought a disreputable if not exactly criminal act, but now people in authority accepted such doings with a smile or a shrug, so I decided to do something similar. The department had retrained me in computer technology, so I knew it was now possible to run a professional consultancy without many filing cabinets and a secretary. Number 2 had also shown me that an office could be run from home. Number 3 had no objection to me setting up my desk and machine in what was then our living room.

"Since you own this house and pay the rates and go out to work each day," I told her, "I'll be the housewife and see to the laundry and cleaning *et cetera.*"

At first she did not mind that arrangement and I was heartily pleased with it because her level of domestic cleanliness was inferior to mine. All she had in common with my first wives was a determination to make the meals we shared.

Despite meeting number 3 through friends of 2, 3's closest friends were very different, being female hospital workers who called themselves The Coven, meeting at least once a week in a public lounge bar and once a fortnight for a party at one of their homes. Most had a husband or male partner who abandoned his home when The Coven convened there. Number 3, weather permitting, held barbecues in her garden, at which times I stayed tactfully indoors. Sometimes one of The Coven strolled in and we chatted. I gathered they preferred me to her previous lover, a doctor who had treated her "rather badly". They also seemed to think me a handy man to have around a house: which made what happened later more surprising.

Housework became the main source of tension between us. It was I who bought the foodstuffs, washed and dried dishes and put them away with the cutlery and cooking utensils so I naturally began arranging the kitchen cupboards and shelves as neatly as possible, throwing out old jars of spices and condiments on the verge of decay, replacing cracked insanitary crockery with clean, modern things. Instead of being pleased she accused me of trying to erase her. She said the same when I ironed her clothes, folded and put them neatly away.

"NOBODY irons clothes nowadays," she yelled, "NOBODY! Chuck them in the airing cupboard like I've always done."

She probably regarded home as a refuge from her highly regulated hospital life. I worked hard and unsuccessfully to stop my cleanliness and order offending her. I could do no kitchen work when she was home because what she called my "virtuous clattering" enraged her.

One day she returned from work frowning thoughtfully and when I asked why said shortly, "Nothing," and when I asked again the following night said, "Just a pain, it doesn't matter."

Strange that a trained nurse belonged to that large class of people who dread

referring their illness to a doctor! Luckily she worked in a hospital. A phone call one day told me she had collapsed and was being operated upon for appendicitis with acute peritonitis. I saw her that evening when she had recovered consciousness and acquired an astonishingly young, fresh, new-born look. I sat silently holding her hand, feeling closer to her than I had felt since our first night together. A month passed before she was fit for home and I visited her at least once a day, would have done so twice every day but her bedside during visiting hours was often crowded with hospital friends so she told me to come in the evenings only.
"What present," I asked myself, "can I give her when she returns home? Of course! A new kitchen."

The renovation carried out by her cheap, quick friend had annoyed me by its awkward shelving, badly hung doors and an old cupboard space walled off with plywood. I imagined many kinds of rot, fungus and insect life burgeoning in there. "Nobody who has been ill," I told myself, "should return to a home with such a probable source of infection in it."

So I had the kitchen completely renovated, expensively and well, with the most modern and easily cleaned equipment, all electric instead of gas. I did not tell her this in hospital, perhaps fooling myself with the notion that she would enjoy the sight of it more when she got home, but of course she at once saw the new kitchen for what it was: a present to me, not her.

"Yes," she said, with a cold little smile, "you've erased me totally now."

I blustered a lot of explanations and apologies then ended by saying that, alas, what had been done could not be undone. She disagreed, saying she could undo it by shifting to a house she could feel at home in – the house of a friend. *This house* was now only legally hers, so she would sell it and if I was the buyer she would subtract the cost of my new kitchen from a surveyor's estimate. I begged her to come to bed with me and talk the matter over next day. She made a phone call, packed some clothing and moved that night to the home of the friend. (I later learned he was the doctor who had been her previous lover.) Her last words to me, or the last words I remember were, "This hasn't been my home since you brought in that bloody machine so you're welcome to it. At a price."

She meant the purchase price of course, with the addition of her complete absence. Did this leave me desolate? Yes. Yes, with a mean little core of satisfaction that for the first time since leaving my parents I would possess a house that was wholly mine. But lying now in the dark with Tilda gently snoring less than two yards from me I started weeping tears I had never shed when number 3 left the house, and when number 2 told me to go to my new woman, and when number 1 said she was divorcing me for another man. I lay weeping for my whole past and could not stop for I suddenly saw what I had never before suspected: that I had lost three splendid women because I had been constantly mean and ungenerous, cold and calculating. Even my lovemaking, I suspected, had not been much more generous than my many acts of solitary masturbation between the marriages. I wept harder than ever. I crawled off the sofa, switched on a lamp and knelt on the floor beside the bed. Tilda stopped snoring, opened her eyes and stared at me.

"Please, Tilda," I said between sobs, "please just let me hold your hand for a while."
Her alarmed look gave way to puzzlement. She withdrew a hand from under the bedclothes and offered it almost shyly. I took it between mine, being careful not to press very hard, then her eyes opened wider as if she was only now clearly seeing me and she muttered, "Don't go away. Always be there."

Then I saw that she needed me, would need nobody *but* me while our lives lasted. With great thankfulness and great contentment, holding her hand, I fell asleep on the floor beside our bed.

PILLOW TALK

WAKENING HE TURNED HIS head and saw she was still reading. After a moment he said,

"About that e-mail you sent."

"I never sent you an e-mail," she said, eyes still on the book.

"Not before today, perhaps, but this afternoon you e-mailed me and said —"

"I repeat," she interrupted, looking hard at him, "I have never sent you or anyone else an e-mail in my life."

"But you did send one to the office this afternoon. I remember it perfectly – the heading stating it was from you to me and everyone else in the firm. Why did you have to tell *them*? You must have sent it from a friend's computer or one in the public library."

"You're still drunk."

"If you mean I was drunk when we came to bed you are wrong. We had only one bottle of wine with the evening meal and I drank only one more glass of it than you. I'm glad you're sorry you sent that message but you'll never persuade me you didn't."

"You're hallucinating. What am I supposed to have said?"

"That you want to leave me. Five words – *I want to leave you* – just that."

She stared at him, shut the book and said bitterly, "Oh, very clever. Cruel, but clever."

"Do you want to leave me?"

"Yes, but I never told you so. I've never told anyone that – they think ours is such a *solid* marriage. You must have noticed it's a farce and this is your bloody cunning way of blaming me for something I never said and was never going to say."

"Blethers!" he cried, "I am *never* cunning, *never* cruel. I remember these words coming up very clear and distinct on the computer screen: *I want to leave you.*"

"Then why didn't you mention it when you came home? Why didn't you mention it over dinner? Are you going to pretend you were brooding over it before we came to bed?"

He thought hard for a while then said,

"You're right. I must have dreamed it before I woke a moment ago."
"I'm glad you've sobered up," she said and resumed reading.

After a while he said, "But you want to leave me."
She sighed and said nothing.
"When will you do it?"
"I don't suppose I'll ever do it," she murmured, still appearing to read, "I haven't the courage to live alone. You're an alcoholic bore but not violent and I'm too old to find anyone better."
"I'm glad!" he said loudly. "I don't want you ever to leave because I love you. My life will be a misery if you leave me."
"Then you're luckier than I am. Go back to sleep."
He turned away from her and tried to sleep. About half an hour later he heard her shut the book and switch off the bedside lamp. He got up and went to a room next door where he had hidden a bottle of whisky for this sort of emergency.

MORAL PHILOSOPHY EXAM

A BIG TELEVISION COMPANY regularly broadcast a news programme informing the viewers of bad deeds: not the bad deeds of corporations who might withdraw advertising revenues, or the bad deeds of big businessmen and government officials who could afford to bring strong libel actions, but the exploitive practices of small private landlords, tradesmen and moneylenders. This did some social good and entertained viewers, who were also encouraged to help the programme by supplying it with evidence of scandalous instances.

So one day the broadcasters heard of a man who liked horses but had become so poor that the few he owned were badly fed and stabled. The broadcasters tried to contact the horses' owner but he hid from them. They besieged his house with a camera crew until he emerged and was filmed fleeing from an interviewer who ran after him shouting unanswered questions. This was broadcast along with distant views of the horses, the faces and voices of concerned neighbours, the comments of a qualified animal doctor. The owner was subsequently charged with cruelty to animals by the Royal Society for Prevention of Cruelty to Animals, was found guilty and jailed for several months as he could not afford to pay a fine. The horses were humanely killed because nobody else wanted them.

Which of the following cared most for the horses?

1 Their owner.
2 The RSPCA.
3 The broadcasters.

Who gained most by these events?

1 Lawyers conducting the trial.
2 The broadcasters.
3 Other horses with incompetent owners.

Who lost most by these events?
1 The owner.
2 The horses.

JOB'S SKIN GAME

FOR GOD'S SAKE DON'T BELIEVE what my wife says: I am still one of the luckiest men who ever walked the earth. Yes of course we've had our troubles, like hundreds and thousands of others recently, and for a while it seemed impossible to carry on. I'd have paid a man to shoot me if I'd known where to find one. But I survived. I recovered. The sun is shining, the birds are singing again, though I perfectly understand why the wife has not recovered and maybe never will.

It was my father who had the really hard life, years and years of it: a joiner's son, self-educated, who after many slips and slides turned a small house-renovation firm into a major building contractor. Before he expired he was a city councillor and playing golf with Reo Stakis. He sent me to the best fee-paying school in Glasgow because "it's there you'll make friends who'll be useful to you in later life", and yes, some were. Not being university material I went straight into the family business and learned it from the bottom up, working as a brickie's labourer for a couple of months on one job, a joiner's labourer on another, a plumber's mate elsewhere and so on till I had first-hand experience of all those jobs and painting, plastering, slating, wiring, the lot. Of course the tradesmen I served knew I was the boss's son. He told them so beforehand and warned them to be as tough on me as on other apprentices. Some were, some weren't. Either way I enjoyed gaining manual skills while using my muscles. I even worked as a navvy for six weeks, and (under supervision, of course) drove a bulldozer and managed a crane. Meanwhile, at night school, I learned the business from a manager's standpoint, while calling in at the firm's head office between whiles to see how it worked at the costing and contracting level. So when the dad collapsed of a stroke I continued the business as if nothing had happened. My mother had died long before so I inherited a fine house in Newton Mearns, a holiday home on Arran and another in the south of Spain.

Is it surprising that I was able to marry the first good-looking woman I fell in love with? She was more than just a pretty face. In business matters she resembled my father more than me. I was less brisk than he in sacking workers when we lacked orders to fully employ them.
"You can't afford to keep men idle," said the wife. I told her that I didn't – that I found them useful though not highly profitable jobs until fresh orders arrived. "Maybe you can afford to do that but your wife and children can't!" she said, using the plural form though still pregnant with our first child, "You're running a modern business, not a charity, and seem anxious to run it into the ground."
I quietened her by signing the family property and private finances over to her on condition that she left the firm to me. It prospered! We sent our boys to the same boarding school as the Prince of Wales.

Being smarter than their old dad they went from there to Glasgow University, then Oxford, then one took to law and the other to accountancy, though both eventually got good posts in a banking house with headquarters in Hong Kong and an office in New York. Alas.

By that time I had sold the main business, being past retiral age. I kept on the small house-renovation firm my dad started with, more as a hobby than anything else. I had always most enjoyed the constructive side of business. Meanwhile the wife, on the advice of her own accountant (not mine) invested our money in a highly respectable dot com pension scheme which she said "will make every penny we own work harder and earn more".
I didn't know what that meant but it sounded convincing until the scheme went bust. Highly respected traders had gambled unsuccessfully with the scheme's assets while spending most of the profits on bonuses for themselves. Clever men, these traders.

But when the fuss died down and the

Newton Mearns house and holiday homes were sold, my wee remaining firm kept us from destitution. We shifted to a three-room flat in the Cowcaddens and without asking help from the boys had everything a respectable couple needs. If some of my wife's friends stopped visiting her she was better without them, I say. And our two highly successful sons in their big New York office were a great consolation to her until, you know, the eleventh of September, you know, and those explosions that look like going on forever.

Years ago I enjoyed a television comedy called *It Ain't Half Hot, Mum* about a British army unit stationed in Burma or Malaya. There was a bearded sage who spouted proverbs representing the Wisdom of the East. One was, "When a man loses all his wealth after contracting leprosy and hearing that his wife has absconded with his best friend, that is no reason for the ceiling not falling on his head." Or as we say in the West, it never rains but it pours. My wife never abandoned me though I sometimes wished she had better company. My efforts to console us drove her wild.

"You must admit," I said, "that compared with most folk in other countries, and many in our own, our lives have been unusually fortunate and comfortable. We must take the rough with the smooth."

"All right for you!" she cried. "What about the boys?"

"After nearly thirty-five very enviable years their only misfortune has been a sudden, unexpected death, and their last few minutes were so astonishing that I doubt if they had time to feel pain."

"They didn't deserve to die!" she shouted.

"Would you be happier if they did?" I asked. "The only evil we should regret is the evil we do. As far as I am aware our sons' firm was not profiting by warfare or industrial pollution. Be glad they died with clean hands."

She stared and said, "Are you telling me to be glad they're dead?"

There is nothing more stupid than trying to talk folk out of natural, heartfelt misery. I had talked to her like some kind of Holy Willie, so I apologised.

After a bath one morning I was towelling myself dry in one of these low beams of sunlight that illuminate tiny specks floating in the air. It let me see something like smoke drifting up from the leg I was rubbing and a shower of tiny white flakes drifting down to the carpet. Like most folk nowadays I know most dust around a house comes from the topmost layer of human skin cells crumbling off while the lower cells replace it. Looking closer I saw the lower layer of skin was more obvious than usual. It reminded me of the sky at night with a few big red far-apart spots like planets, and clusters of smaller ones between them like constellations, and areas of cloudy pinkness which, peered at closely, were made by hundreds of tiny little spots like stars in the Milky Way. Then came itching and scratching. The first is widely supposed to cause the second but in my experience this is only partly true. The first itch was so tiny that a quick stab with a needle could have stopped it had I known the exact point to stab. But this was impossible, so I scratched the general area which itched even more the harder, the more widely and wildly I scratched. This crescendo of itching and scratching grew so fiercely ecstatic that I only stopped when my nails had torn bloody gashes in that leg and the delight changed to pain.

Since then I have often enjoyed that ecstasy, suffered that pain. The disease spread to other limbs, torso, neck and head. I could no longer supervise work in houses under renovation. Dust from cement, plasterboard and timber maddened my itches to a frenzy that only the hottest of baths subdued. Under the pain of scalding water the skin also felt many wee points of delight, as if each itch was being exactly, simultaneously scratched and satisfied. I left the bath with my skin a patchwork of pink and red sores that I patted dry, ointmented with Vaseline, covered with clean pyjamas, every itch now replaced by dull pain. So I went to bed and slept sound by quickly drinking half a litre of neat spirits. Perhaps modern pills would have knocked me out more cheaply but I felt safer with a drug folk have tested on themselves for centuries.

So the main side effects of the disease are:
(1) exile from the constructive part of my business,
(2) exile from my wife's bed,

(3) her endless work to clean up my stained sheets and underclothes,
(4) greatly increased dependence on alchohol,
(5) a search for cures.

After a thing called A Patch Test my doctor explained that the disease was due to an inherited defect in the immune system defending my skin. A mainly serene and prosperous life had not strained it but now, weakened by recent emotional shocks, I was allergic to forms of dust that nobody could avoid. The origin of the allergy, being genetic, was incurable, but medication should reduce the symptoms. He prescribed a steroid cream to combat eruptions, an emollient to reduce the flaking, anti-histamine pills to ease the itching and (to be used instead of soap) a bath oil that also counteracted infection.

These helped for a while. The rashes healed in places and itched far less until the steroid cream ran out. My doctor was unwilling to prescribe more because continuous use made the skin dangerously thin. He prescribed a less potent antibiotic cream and arranged a consultation with a skin specialist who, because of a long waiting list, would see me five months later. My wife wanted me to jump that queue by paying for a private consultation. I refused for two reasons.

(1) I am a socialist who thinks our national health service is the best thing the British Government ever created, and is undermined by folk buying into a private system which can only exist because its doctors are also partly subsidised by ordinary taxpayers, and:
(2) I like saving money.

But while waiting for the appointment I noticed near my home an alternative medicine clinic, though not the sort using astrology and occultism. The consultation fee was not huge so I tried it. An ordinary looking youth weighed me, examined my fingernails, tongue and inner eyelids, asked questions about my eating and drinking habits, then delivered a small lecture.

Everyone must live by consuming more solids and fluids than their body needs, so our digestions, kidneys and liver help to excrete what cannot nourish us. With age these weaken and work less efficiently, especially in middle-class people like me who eat and drink too much. The excess not expelled through my bowels and bladder is retained in fat or expelled through the skin, damaging it on the way. I should therefore stop drinking alcohol, coffee and tea, apart from one cup of the last each day. I should daily drink at least three pints of pure water, should stop eating meat and poultry, but consume as much fish as I liked if it was not fried. I should also cut out dairy produce – eggs, milk, butter, cheese – also sugar and salt, but eat more fruit and vegetables, preferably organically grown. Two months of this diet would heal my skin if I also took more exercise: a brisk half-hour daily walk would be sufficient. When cured I could experiment by trying some things I had eliminated – wine with my meals or ham-and-egg breakfasts. If the disease returned I would then know what to blame. He also prophesied that any orthodox skin specialist I saw would prescribe a stronger kind of steroid ointment than prescribed by my general practitioner.

I left that clinic certain I had been told the truth and determined not to inform my wife. She would have adopted that diet for me with enthusiasm, especially the no-alcohol part; I would then have started tippling in secret and been continually found out and denounced. But I told her when I visited a Chinese clinic that sold me brown paper bags containing mixtures of dry twigs, fronds and fungus with instructions to boil the contents of one bag in water – simmer for half an hour – strain off the liquid – drink a cupful three times a day for two days then repeat the process with the next bag. My wife refused to do that so I did it myself, but kept forgetting to set the cooker alarm so twice ruined pans by boiling the vegetation into adhesive cinders. I realised that orthodox British medicine was the most convenient, even when the skin specialist prescribed what the nature healer had foretold. Luckily by then I had turned my bad skin into a hobby.

Explanation at this point becomes embarrassing because it requires a four letter word I hate. Chamber's Dictionary gives it several meanings but the relevant one is this:

Scab *noun:* a **crust formed over a sore or wound**.

I take a gentle pleasure in carefully removing most such crusts and have my own names for the main varieties:

Cakes and Crumbs. Black or brown lumps that form on the deepest scratches. Dried blood is a main ingredient. I try not to touch these because, picked off too soon, they leave a hole in which fresh blood wells up before clotting.

Hats. A cake or crumb may grow a crisp white border, as much part of it as a brim is part of a hat. This brim overlaps the surrounding skin in such a way that the tip of a fingernail, slid beneath, easily lifts off the whole hat uncovering a moist but shallow and unbleeding wound. A few hours later other kinds of crust form over that. They also form over larger sores where topskin has crumbled off, flaked off or been scratched off.

Bee-wing. Pale grey and gauzy. It has white lines like veins on wings of bees, wasps and house flies, but more random looking. Minute red or brown spots sometimes suggest wings of more exotic insects. Bee-wing is so transparent that if laid on a printed page words can be read through it.

Parchment. Pale yellowish-brown, not

gauzy, yet as transparent as bee-wing. It seems made by the drying of moisture exuded from raw skin beneath. I remove it by pressing a fingertip into the skin on each side and pulling them apart. The living underskin stretches, the parchment splits, its edges curling up like the edges of water lily leaves, making peeling off easy.
Moss. This yellowish-grey furriness seems an intruder, like the mould on rotten fruit. It grows in circular holes and narrow grooves made by accidental scratches in swollen, inflamed skin, but is so far below the skin's level that fingernails cannot reach it without doing more damage. I use fine-pointed tweezers to grip an edge of such growths and, since their roots must be intertwined, easily lift out the whole mossy mat or strip.
Paper. A splendid example of this lost me control of my remaining firm.

The board meeting in our Waterloo Street office consisted of secretary, accountant, lawyer, works supervisor and two major shareholders who were partners from the days when my father's firm had built housing schemes. As chairman I let the others do most of the talking, usually sitting with closed eyes and even dozing a little until silence fell. Then I would sit up, summarise the situation in a few crisp words, indicate the only sensible choices, hold a vote on them, then ask the secretary to announce the next item on our agenda. One afternoon, halfway through a meeting, I sensed that my left arm was in a very interesting state. I excused myself, went to lavatory, sat on pan, rolled up shirtsleeve. A big expanse of skin inside the elbow joint had withered into dry white paperiness, paperiness so brittle that it had cracked into little four-sided lozenges like an area of neatly laid marquetry. And it was NOT ALIVE. My first impulse was to set fingernails of my right hand in line and use them to rake that dead paper off with two or three sweeping strokes. It would have left an area of raw underskin with bleeding gashes in it and many wee triangular paper scraps standing up and not easy to nip off. So with the tweezers I delicately prized off each paper tile and placed it between the pages of my pocket book, leaving a raw but undamaged area on which I spread an ointment prescribed by the specialist – Betnovate or

Trimovate or Eumovate, I forget which. Then I rolled down sleeve, washed hands, returned to meeting. While performing that delicate operation I was perfectly happy.

"Well, gents, what have you been discussing?" I said, having been absent for ten or twenty minutes. Only the secretary looked straight at me. The rest seemed too embarrassed to look at anything but the table before them, then they looked furtively at the works supervisor. He was the youngest, the one I most liked and trusted because I had promoted him from being a site foreman. He cleared his throat then explained that, though he did not wholly agree with the rest of the board, there was a general feeling that I should leave the firm's steering wheel and become more of a back-seat driver; my great experience would always be valuable but blah blah blah blah *et cetera*. I grinned as I heard all this and when he fell silent was about to quell the mutiny – could easily have done it – but was suddenly overtaken by weariness with the whole business. It occurred to me also that someone had sampled the clear liquid in the tumbler beside my notepad and found it was not

water but Polish vodka. I sipped from it, shrugged and said, "Have it your own way gents."
All but the works supervisor at once cheered up, congratulated me on my wise decision, said I would gain rather than lose financially because blah blah blah blah blah. So the paperish arm left me with nothing to enjoy but my skin game.

The nature of other crusts (**Lace**, **Fish-scale**, **Snakeskin**, **Shell**, **Biscuit**, **Straw** and **Pads**) I leave to the imagination of my readers, but some cannot be classified by a simple name. From the shallow valley above the caudal vertebrae I have removed three discs of the same size but different textures: beewing, parchment and paper, joined at a point where they overlapped by a little dark purple oval cake. I have also detached something like a tiny withered leaf, intricately mottled with black and grey, glossily smooth on the underside but with a knap like Lilliputian velvet on the upper. Anything often thought about enters our dreams and I sometimes dream of more extravagant growths. One is like a thin slab of soft, colourless cheese, slightly wrinkled: it peels off with no physical sensation at all. Another lies under it and another under that. At last I uncover what I know is the lowest layer which I fear to remove, knowing that underneath lies nothing but bone wrapped in a network of naked veins, arteries, tendons and nerves, yet intense curiosity is driving me to expose what I dread to see when I fortunately awaken.

I reduced the bouts of wild scratching to once a week and between them carefully removed the crusts I have listed and the others I have not. The pleasure of this harvesting is twofold: *sensual* because the raw skin beneath feels briefly relieved, perhaps because it can perspire and breathe more freely; *emotional* because I like separating the dead from the quick, removing what is not the living me from what is. After each session I apply ointment then sweep up the dust, flakes and crusts with a hand-held vacuum cleaner of the sort used on car upholstery. Yet I do so with a kind of regret, feeling these former growths of mine should be *used* for something. I considered gathering the biggest in a porcelain jar as Victorian ladies gathered flower petals, but the scent would not have been sweet. So instead of that —

I switch a plate of the electric cooker to maximum heat and with the tweezers lay on it a little pagoda-like tower of the largest crusts. They catch fire, each glowing red-hot before, with a faint sizzle, darkening and merging with the rest in a small black wart or bubble that heaves as if trying to rise off the plate, then collapses into a smear of white ash while releasing a wisp of smoke. This wisp, inhaled, has a tiny but definite odour of roasted meat. Surely this sight, sound and smell are as near as I can get to enjoying my cremation while alive? The ceremony is performed, of course, when my wife is away from home, but it once engrossed me so completely that I did not notice she had returned and was watching.

"What are you doing?"

Lacking the strength to stay silent and the energy to lie, I told her.

"But why?"

"Because I enjoy it."

She arranged for me to see a psychotherapist.

He is a grave person not much younger than me. The following short summary of five politely laborious conversations makes them seem like comedy cross-talk with him the straight man, me the joker. A first person narrative makes such distortions inevitable.

I began by saying I had only come to please my wife and doubted if he could help me, as the skin game was a harmless way of getting fun out of an incurable illness.

"But was the disease not caused by huge financial loss and the deaths of your sons? And have you not since become something of an alcoholic?"

I admitted that my illness had a psychological element. We then conversed as if it was the only element, because of course I was paying him to do that. He asked about my sex life. I said that like most faithful married men of my age and class and nation I had outgrown it.

"But has your wife? And do you not see that these obsessive scratchings and pickings are a regression to pre-adolescent infantilism?"

I agreed that I had reverted to infantilism

but said I preferred the older name of second childhood, a condition to be expected in a man over sixty. My childish skin game perhaps blended narcissism, pre-masturbatory sado-masochism and a form of transferred coprophilia (I enjoyed coming back at him with big words) but it harmed nobody. I was sorry that my wife could not sleep with a man in my state but would not complain if she began visiting massage parlours or took up with a healthier lover, though in a woman of her age, class and nation this was improbable.
"Does it not occur to you that this narcissistic sado-masochism (as you agree to call it), this fast or slow flaying of your own epidermis – is a kind of self-punishment? What do you punish yourself for? Where lies your subconscious guilt?"
I could not tell him so he told me.

At first he suggested I was subconsciously glad my sons had died, so felt subconsciously guilty of murdering them. I admitted that since their boarding-school days I had never felt at ease with the boys because (though they tried to hide it) they seemed to find my voice and manners too plebeian, but I was glad – not angry – that they felt happier with their mother than with me. Their deaths were surely depressing enough without making me a subconscious murderer.

Then he tackled me from the Marxist angle. I had once been nearly a millionaire and surely nobody innocently grows as rich as that? He was right, in a way. In the building trade a lot of contracts are won by private deals that bypass the advertised requests for tenders. Not many such deals involve the transfer of banknotes in plain envelopes. What outsiders call corruption is more a matter of people above a certain income level exchanging useful social favours, and certainly my father got business that way. I avoided these deals, which was not easy at first. A noted Lord Provost felt personally insulted when I ignored his hints that my bids for contracts would be accepted if submitted in particular terms on particular mornings. That was why I did not become a millionaire. I may have inherited some ill-gotten gains but had never resented paying income tax, and when that was reduced by Thatcher's government I more than made up for what I owed the human race in standing orders of money steadily paid to Oxfam, Amnesty International, Greenpeace and Scottish Wildlife. Despite a reduced income I still pay several of these orders. It is conscience money so I am at peace with my conscience.

The therapist could not believe that, so asked about my religion. I told him my mother had been a Catholic expelled from her local chapel when she married a Protestant, though my dad was not a church-going Protestant. His religion was money-making. To do so he congregated eagerly with Freemasons and Jesuits, Orangemen and Knights of Saint Columba. In Newton Mearns my wife attended a local Episcopalian Church, unlike me, though I had been friendly with her minister or vicar or whatever he was called: a decent man and one of the few Newton Mearns lot who still visited us. Like many non-religious folk I had a loose faith in a kind of God who was benign rather than punitive. I assumed God had the difficult job of managing the universe in ways that could not satisfy everybody. After all, He had made millions of microbes and insects that could only thrive by killing millions of bigger animals and we had given Him no good reason to prefer people to other forms of life. I was being deliberately provocative when I said that. Small signs had led me to think this soul-doctor, despite his Freudian jargon, was a Believer, though probably in a Jewish, Catholic or Protestant God rather than a Hindu or Mahomedan one.

"I have read," (I added) "that even in our cleanest buildings the carpets and the upholstery contain whole nations of wee beasts fed by the protein from old, discarded skin. I must have more than doubled the population of such beasties in my house. Their delight in the nourishment my eczema showers on them may compensate God for the pain it gives my wife."

With an effort my soul-healer kept his temper and said that many neurotic self-justifers made gods in their own image, but mine was the nastiest he had encountered. I disagreed, saying mine was a harmless image – nobody would kill or strike another in defence of it.

"But arguing about God," I told him, "is as futile as arguing with God. Let us agree that his mercy and justice are beyond any understanding. Goodbye and good luck."

That was a week ago and I'm not going back to him, though I feel our little chats did me good.

This morning I dreamed of wakening and lying naked on top of the bed, unable to move even a finger because my whole skin had stiffened into a hard rigid sheath. With a mighty effort I at last heaved myself up, feeling a delicious pang as the sheath cracked all over. Looking down I saw myself clad in a mosaic of parchment patches that began to move apart as their edges curled upward making them easy to pluck off. And what lay beneath was *not* raw cuticle but clean healthy skin. I awoke and found this was not so, but now believe that one day my skin will heal as unexpectedly as it diseased. Meanwhile my wee house-renovation firm, even without my controlling hand, is doing very well.

It will soon be quite a big firm again,
thank God.

MISS KINCAID'S AUTUMN

WHEN LOCAL NICKNAMES were common I grew up in a place we called The Long Town, a name not printed on maps or railway timetables. It had council houses where coal miners lived, a high street of properties rented by our shopkeepers and tradesmen, and several mansions and bungalows owned by so few professional folk that everyone in the town knew them. Conversations about local affairs usually mentioned Big Tam Kincaid the Free Kirk Minister, also his son Big Sam, schoolteacher and Labour councillor. I knew both by sight, the first as a gaunt striding figure in the streets, the second as a stout one crossing the school playground. I was never Big Sam's pupil but often heard his voice booming from an adjacent classroom. Joe Kincaid, a second son, was of usual height but in the merchant navy so hardly ever seen. Almost as invisible were Poor Mrs Kincaid and a daughter, Wee Chrissie, who were only mentioned in women's conversations. When I asked why Mrs Kincaid was Poor my mother said, "Her men need a lot of her attention."

I left The Long Town for university when television aerials had sprouted on most rooftops and the cinema had become a bingo hall. A job and a marriage kept me away from it but I often returned to visit my parents so saw the town change like the rest of Scotland. The railway and colliery closed. Cars and unemployment increased. Council houses took on a slummier look. At the edge of the town arose an estate of private houses, each with a garden and garage facing a circular drive. To discourage outsiders, it had only one way in, no through road and no shops, but it brought little extra business to the high street. The owners were commuters who mostly shopped in Glasgow or Edinburgh, where they worked. The wee shops of my childhood (baker, grocer, draper, sweet shop, newsagent, cobbler, clock mender) became mini-markets or shut forever.

I also heard that Poor Mrs Kincaid died, leaving Wee Chrissie as housekeeper. Big Sam became a headmaster, married one of his staff and brought her to live in the Free Kirk manse where his father was now a bedridden invalid. Soon after the wedding Sam's wife left him and a stroke paralysed his legs, events so close together that gossip differed on which came first. Though confined to a wheelchair Big Sam fought bravely to keep his jobs as headmaster and local councillor. Having many sympathisers he succeeded for a while, but misfortunes had destroyed the joviality that had made his bullying ways bearable. Former colleagues joined with enemies and forced him to resign from both jobs. These colleagues had been his only friends; he now regarded them as traitors. Then his father died, leaving Sam alone with Wee Chrissie in the former manse. I asked if she had no friends.

"I never hear of Miss Kincaid having visitors," said my mother in a way that showed the nickname was not now appropriate, "though nobody dislikes her."

I got divorced and between jobs lived with my parents for a whole summer. Single women visiting Long Town pubs were looked at with grave suspicion. I dislike bingo so joined an evening class on modern Scots literature held in the public library. The lecturer was an enthusiast who tried hard to hide a conviction that the best things about his subject had been his meetings with the authors who wrote it. When he failed to do so I sensed that a straight-faced woman beside me was trembling. I glanced at her sideways. She gave me a smile that showed she was holding in tremendous laughter. I smiled back.

We left the library together, fell into conversation and I was surprised to learn she was Chrissie Kincaid, whom I had always imagined a poor wee timorous beastie. This woman was as tall as most of us who don't wear high heeled shoes. She

was quiet and self-contained but keenly observant, with highly independent and broadminded views. Our parental homes lay in the same direction so I invited her back for tea. She sighed and said, "Alas, no. I regret my early training but it has made it impossible for me – a Kincaid! – to accept hospitality I cannot return."
"Then return it. I'll take tea in your house any day."
"No you won't."
"Why not?"
"I can't tell you because Kincaids never explain family matters to outsiders. Nor can we meet in a pub because female Kincaids don't drink alcohol in public. Nor can we meet in a tearoom or café because The Long Town hasn't one nowadays. But I hope you and I have another talk after the next evening class."

Curiosity drove me to see her sooner. I had offered to lend a book. Two days later I took it to the former manse, a solid grey stately Victorian building with a tall monkey puzzle tree on the lawn. A brass bell handle, pulled, made a distant dolorous clanging somewhere inside. Two minutes later Miss Kincaid opened the

door and looked at me with raised eyebrows. I gave her the book and was saying something about it when a great voice from behind her said, "No whispering! No secrets from me, Chrissie! Bring your friend in."
It was a voice I remembered from childhood, booming but distinct and able to penetrate walls without yelling. Miss Kincaid shrugged her shoulders and ushered me in.

We crossed a dark lobby with a staircase and entered a very warm room of dark furniture with a bright coal fire. Beside it in a wheelchair sat Big Sam, now hideously fat, his legs covered by a tartan rug. A table at his elbow had books and papers on it, a jug of water, a glass and a decanter of pale golden liquid. He said, "Your name is? Valerio? Formerly Ferguson? Then your father had the excellent dry goods shop on the high street. I taught your uncles and your elder brother. Chrissie, offer our Mrs Valerio biscuits, cake and – tea? Coffee? Sherry? Why not sherry? I, you see, am a whiskyholic" – (he waved toward the decanter) – "but I never drink enough to become a total victim of my sister's ministrations. No. I am careful to keep my

mind intact, my intellect in control."
I said I would like tea and Miss Kincaid left the room.
"Good!" he said on a more intimate note, "I am a crippled giant but not the ogre my sister has probably suggested to you. My sufferings derive from a strong intelligence diverted by those who hate me into the cul-de-sac of memory – a form of torture I assure you, Mrs Valerio. What a relief to meet someone with whom I can intelligently converse!"

He talked to me for a very long time. Miss Kincaid must have brought biscuits and tea but his flow of talk wiped out any sense of consuming them. He told me the social history of The Long Town in the lifetime of his father and himself, illustrating it with personal anecdotes, many of them interesting, but it is exhausting to be treated as an audience for over an hour by a single intense speaker. The more often I looked at the clock the more often he asked if he was boring me. I lacked the courage to answer truly but he was watching me far too closely to miss other signs of restlessness. They inspired him to talk faster and faster.

Miss Kincaid must have learned not to hear Sam when not wanting to. She sat nearby calmly reading with a slight smile on her face that first struck me as mischievous then downright malicious until, after ninety minutes, she snapped the book shut, stood up and said, "Mrs Valerio has to visit some other people, Sam."

I stood up too.

"Goodbye, Mrs Valerio," he said, offering his hand. "I am at the mercy of a sister who is given to engineering these abrupt departures. My little holiday is ended but please visit the crippled giant again. Come again soon. Don't be a stranger."

I said I would come again. With something like a sneer he reached for the whisky muttering what sounded like, "I doubt it." Miss Kincaid escorted me to the front door murmuring, "Serves you right," but our later walks back from the evening class were as friendly as the first.

Years later I returned to The Long Town for my father's funeral, then for my mother's. Both had Church of Scotland services. The second was better attended because the Free Kirk congregation had by then joined ours, having become too small to maintain a separate minister of its own. I knew hardly any of the old people present so on leaving the church was pleased to see Miss Kincaid looking remarkably unchanged. I told her so and asked about her brother.

"Here he is!" she said, introducing a small compact man with eyes as blue and alert as her own. The complexion of his bald head and cut of his neatly trimmed beard showed this was Joe, the nautical brother. I asked how Sam was.

"As vocal as ever," she said merrily. "We've moved him upstairs. Come home for a drink with us."

So we three walked back to the old manse.

It was a chill November afternoon with occasional gusts of thin rain and I made a conventional remark about the weather.

"Yes, a miserable climate," said Joe cheerily. "I've seen much worse weather but for sheer dull depressing misery a damp Scottish November cannot be surpassed."

He seemed highly satisfied with such Scottish Novembers.

"I disagree," said Miss Kincaid. "Autumn

is Scotland's most colourful season. Fresh spring leaves look lovely but they don't look fresh for long. By the end of summer they've been tired and dusty for months. Then comes September and they start withering into golden greens, deep purples and all the rich colours I've seen in reproductions of Gauguin's paintings. I'm sure they would damage our eyes if we saw them by the strong sunlight of Tahiti."

"Those don't look very dazzling," said Joe, pointing to the pavement. Adhering to the tarmac and almost as black was a thin carpet of rotten old leaves with some recent ones the colour of dung.

"But what an excellent background for those!" said Miss Kincaid, pointing to a couple of fallen chestnut fans further on. Each leaf was a glowing yellow that blended through orange into crimson at the tip, with a pale green streak along the central veins.

As we entered the manse lobby we heard from above a vocal hullabaloo. Miss Kincaid looked at Joe who said calmly, "Yes, it's my turn."

Without haste he removed and hung up cap and coat and went upstairs. Miss Kincaid led me into the room where I had last seen Sam, switching on bright lights that made the dark furniture look solidly comforting instead of forbidding. The air was pleasantly warm.

"Home," she said. "Home home home. Would you like a sherry? I'm having one."

We sat sipping sherry and watching the flames in the hearth. She said, "They're gas flames now and no trouble at all. Sam loved the old coal fire, said the constantly changing flames were a more varied show than television. He also liked to see me poking it or adding coals every half hour. When Joe came home we outnumbered Sam. Our change to gas so enraged him that he retreated upstairs. We installed a lift attachment to the banister that can easily take the twenty stone of him up and down. Joe would gladly drive Sam and his wheelchair to the park or anywhere else he likes, but no. Sam says he will never let anyone see a Kincaid in a pitiable state, will never let Joe condescend to him, so he sticks in his room. Laziness masquerading as pride, you see. Sheer obstinate idiocy in fact. Yet Sam used to be a better Labour councillor than most of them."

We had another sherry. She said, "Our

father is to blame. He was a selfish monster who forbad us to play with other children. He damaged Sam most because Sam was his favourite so grew up like him, only happy with people he could bully. Thank God Joe and I had each other. We told each other all sorts of lovely stories and invented all sorts of exciting games when nobody was looking. Our affection made us quite unfit for matrimony. By going to sea Joe was able to sample other sorts of affection. He told me about them in letters because he knew I could never be jealous of purely temporary mates. He was living the life I would have led had I been a man, and I knew he would return to me at last. Another sherry?"

Joe entered and said, "Dinner-time. The Great I Am upstairs has grudgingly assented to oxtail soup, bangers and mash, tinned peaches with ice cream. What do you ladies want?"

We wanted the same. Joe prepared it and the three of us dined at the kitchen table with long chatty intervals between courses, the last of which was coffee with chocolates and liqueurs. Prompted by Chrissie Joe quietly recounted very entertaining comic or terrifying oversea adventures and every forty minutes he or she went upstairs and attended briefly to Sam. Sitting round the kitchen table was so agreeable that we ended the evening there playing scrabble. My companions showed a relaxed pleasure in each other that I have sometimes (not often) noticed in recently married couples, but such marital pleasure is usually exclusive. I felt part of this Kincaid domesticity and had not felt so happily at home for years.

I told Miss Kincaid so when I was leaving. I think she replied that Autumn could be quite a satisfactory season, but being tipsy I may have imagined that.

MY EX HUSBAND

I WAS NINETEEN WHEN COLIN and I met at a friend's party. He was nearly the same age and had a job in the navy. Though not in uniform and not remarkably handsome he was well dressed and carried himself handsomely without seeming arrogant. His conversation was good humoured, with a pleasant touch of shyness. He was also interested in me: the first to be interested since my father's death seven years earlier. We decided to marry. I had a good secretarial job. We raised a joint loan that let us buy a nice house in a pleasant street.

Shortly before the wedding I discovered he expected me to marry his mother too, so was terrified by the thought that our marriage might be a lasting one. In 1960s Scotland this was not an absurd idea. At that time the law made divorces too expensive to be usual in working-class districts where the few divorced men were widely pitied because they must now cook their own meals and wash their own clothes. The divorced women were thought easy meat by men and public dangers by other women. I hated the idea of a divorce but knew I could not live till death parted us with a man who expected me to eat with his relations. I had no mother, having been orphaned in my teens. My only relatives were two aunts who prided themselves on their intelligence and avoided me because I was cleverer than their own children. I was therefore shocked to find Colin expected us to visit his mother almost every night of the week and his married sister every weekend. He said the meals they made were more normal than mine. Here is an example of that normal.

Chicken Soup, made by boiling a chicken in water with salt but nothing else. The resulting liquid, ladled into deep plates, had a layer of chicken fat on top. I made a hole in this with my spoon and tried to drink the soup through it, but the layer of fat still kept the fluid underneath scalding. It had to be sipped slowly: so slowly that when the bird's carcass arrived as a main course it was nearly cold. As were the sprouts and totties served with it. As were the tart and congealed custard that followed. The meal was also delayed by my mother-in-law or her daughter washing, drying and putting away the last course's cutlery before serving the next. They did that swiftly, but to enjoy some remaining warmth in the second and third courses we had to eat them at a gallop. Despite causes of delay I once shared a family Christmas dinner, with crackers and funny paper hats, where three courses and every sign of us having eaten them vanished in half an hour.

Perhaps that was the kind of food and way of eating Colin enjoyed at sea. I could not provide such normality and refused to eat with his family more than once a week. I tried persuading him to dine with me in Italian, Indian and Chinese restaurants, but he found them too exotic. I suppose our marriage lasted for years because he was usually at sea. When at home – I mean the home we shared – he usually watched television while sipping lager in our sitting room. We only quarreled once. Friends had visited me on a local political matter. The television was playing at a low volume so I exchanged a few quiet words with them in a corner of the room. After they left Colin declared that, before inviting others in, I should have picked up and hidden the empty beer cans he had strewn over the carpet. I pointed out that I was a wage-earner like himself, not a house serf like his mother.

Soon after this he moved back in with her, having left the navy and found work in our town as a security guard. She was certainly tidier than me. Divorce in Scotland was now as cheap and frequent as in other places, so we divorced. I raised another bank loan and paid him for his share of the house. I heard later that he bought a flashy car, a Reliant Scimitar with the money, but never told his mother where he got it, so she came to think I had cheated him. That is my only grudge against him.

Thank goodness we had no children.

SINKINGS

SUCCESS IS OVERRATED. The best proof of our worth is how we respond to failure. Herman Melville said that or something very like it. My marital partner still loves me, so do our children, I have recently retired with a cosy pension from a professional job which did some good and very little harm, so I have never been tested by really big failures. Yet the moments I remember with most interest are not my happiest ones, but those times when the ordinary ground under my feet seemed suddenly to sink, leaving me several yards lower than I thought normal or possible. This lower level did not prevent pleasures I had enjoyed at higher ones, but the pleasure never seemed to raise me up again. These sinkings (depressions is too mild a word for them) were never caused by irrevocable disasters, like the death of a parent. I am no masochist, but disasters on that scale stimulated and bucked me up. What let me down worst were failures of common decency, especially the first two.

My father was a businessman who died leaving just enough money for mother to send me to what was thought a very grand boarding school – the sons of many rich, well-known people went there. My immediate dislike of the place on arrival increased with time. The sons of the rich and famous were a social élite to which the teachers also belonged. Boys without much pocket money were excluded unless a brilliant appearance or talent for sport or clowning got them "taken up" by the smart majority. I belonged to a minority who were not physically bullied but usually treated as if invisible. I suppose if we had not existed the rest could not have felt so exclusive and fashionable. If we invisibles had united we would have formed a class more exclusive than the rest because smaller, but we despised ourselves too much to do that.

I had one friend among the élite, or

thought I had: a senior military man's son. He enjoyed modern American literature as much as I did. We never noticed each other when he was with his fashionable friends, but on meeting apart from them in the school library we sometimes went walks together chattering enthusiastically about books whose main characters rebelled against social codes of a type that seemed to rule our own institution. Our form of rebellion was to identify various teachers and head boys with the deranged bullies and conformists of *Catch-22, Catcher in the Rye, Portnoy's Complaint.* Doing so often reduced us to fits of helpless laughter. Our homes in Glasgow were the only other thing we had in common. At the start of a summer holiday we exchanged addresses.

I phoned him a fortnight later and suggested we meet in town.
"I've a better idea," he said, "You come over here. Come this afternoon. I'm having a kind of a party . . ."
He hesitated then added, "As a matter of fact it's my birthday."
I thanked him and asked if it would be a very smart occasion? He said,"No no no, just come the way you are."

He lived in Pollokshields, south of the river, and I arrived with a copy of *Slaughterhouse 5* in my pocket, a book I knew he would enjoy. I had never before visited a mansion standing in its own grounds. I pressed the bell and after a while the door was opened by an elderly woman in a black gown who stared at me, frowning. I said, "Is Raymond in?"

She walked away. It seemed foolish to remain on the doormat so I stepped inside, closing the door behind me. The hall had a mosaic floor, a huge clock, corridors and a broad staircase leading out between Roman-looking pillars. I stood there listening hard for sounds of a party and could hear nothing at all. A tall man with a military moustache entered and said very gently, "Yes?"

"Is Raymond in?"

He said "I'll see about that," and went away. A lot of time passed. The clock struck a quarter hour. I sat down on the slightly rounded top of an antique ebony chest and noticed the time pass, feeling more and more bewildered. Fifteen minutes later the tall man appeared again, stared at me, said, "Why are you still sitting there looking so miserable? Get out! *We* don't want you."

He opened the front door and I walked through it.

That was my first and worst sinking, also the end of my friendship with Raymond. I planned to studiously ignore him when our paths next crossed in the school library, but I never saw him there again.

The second sinking was a milder affair on my last day at that school. I stood with eight or nine other leavers, Raymond among them, in the Headmaster's study, pretending to absorb a flow of the man's brisk, facile, foreseeable, completely uninteresting platitudes. He ended with a firm, "Goodbye and good luck gentlemen. And Gilliland, stay behind for a moment."
He shook hands with the rest who left and I remained feeling rather puzzled, because this was the first time he had ever spoken to me. He sat behind his desk, clasped his hands upon it, looked at me sternly over them for a while then said, "Don't forget, Gilliland, that syphilis is an absolute killer. You can go now."
So I went.

Why did he talk as if *I* was a sexual maniac? Why was I the only school leaver he said that to? As in all single sex schools for adolescents there had been discreet homosexual liaisons among us, but not among us in the invisible class – we were too demoralised to enjoy anything but the most solitary kind of sex. Was it possible that my slightly secretive walks with Raymond had been noticed disapprovingly by his other friends and reported to the teachers? Was our laughter over the antics of Portnoy and Yossarian overheard and interpreted as something sexually and socially dangerous? Was this reported to his father? And was keeping me behind to make that inane remark a headmaster's ploy to avoid shaking an unpopular pupil's hand?

I don't know, but if so Britain is
a very queer nation.

AIBLINS

LONG AGO A COLLEGE OF further education paid me to help folk write poems, stories and other things that bring nobody a steady wage. I had applied for the job because I was in debt and needed a steady wage. The college also provided an office, desk, two chairs and flow of hopeful writers who met me one at a time. I must have talked to nearly a hundred of them while the job lasted but can now only remember:

(1) A shy housewife writing a novel about being the mistress of a South American dictator.

(2) An engineering lecturer writing a TV comedy about lecturers in a college of further education.

(3) Two teenage girls, unknown to each

other, who wrote passionate verses against the evils of abortion.

(4) A dauntingly erudite medical student writing a dissertation proving, by Marxist dialectic, that Rimsky Korsakov's *Golden Cockerel* was a better forecast of mankind's political future than Wagner's *Ring*.

(5) The twelve-year-old daughter of Chinese restaurateurs who, led in by an older sister or perhaps mother or aunt, gravely handed me a sheaf of papers with a narrow column of small neat writing down the middle of each, writing that tersely described such horribly possible events that I feared they were cries for help, though of course I treated them as fiction.

(6) And Ian Gentle.

Ian was a thin student whose manner suggested he found life a desperate but comical game he was bound to lose. He gave me a page of prose telling how raindrops slide down leaves and stems, then join between grass blades in trickles that gradually fill hollows in the ground making them pools, pools steadily enlarging until they too join and turn fields into lakes. Without emotional adverbs and adjectives, without surprising metaphors, similes or dramatic punctuation, Gentle's ordinary words made a natural event seem rare and lovely. My new job had not yet taught me caution. I looked across the desk, waved the page of prose at him and said, "If I had written this I would strongly suspect myself of genius."

He smiled slyly and asked, "Can I sell it?"

"No. Too short. If you made it part of a story with the rest equally good *Chapman* might print it but Scottish magazines pay very little. Even in England the best literary magazines pay less for a story than a shop assistant's weekly wage. But this is a beautiful description, perfect in itself. Write more of them."

He shrugged hopelessly and said, "I can't. You see I was inspired when I wrote that."

"What inspired you?"

"Something I heard by accident. I switched on the radio one night and heard this bloke, Peter Redgrove, spouting his poetry, very weird stuff. I'm not usually fond of poetry but this was different. There was a lot of water in what he recited and I'm fond of grey days with the rain falling steadily like I often saw it on my granny's farm when I was a wee boy. I suddenly wanted to write like Peter Redgrove, not describing water behaving weirdly but water doing the sort of things I used to notice and like."

"If a short burst of good poetry has this effect on you then expose yourself to more. There are several books of Redgrove's poetry. Read all of them, then read MacCaig, Yeats, Frost, Carlos Williams, Auden, Hardy, Owens —"

"Why bother?"

"You might enjoy them."

"But what would it lead to?"

"If they inspired you to write more prose of this quality . . . and if you persisted with your writing, and got some of it into magazines . . . eventually, at the age of forty, you could end up sitting behind a desk like me talking to somebody like you."

He giggled, apologised and asked if nobody in Scotland earned a living by writing. I told him that a few writers of historical romance, crime fiction, science fiction and love stories earned the equivalent of a teacher's income by writing a new novel every year or two.

"Thanks," said Gentle standing up to leave, "I don't think I'll bother. But if it's

genius you want read Luke Aiblins's stuff. It's as weird as Redgrove's."
"Is he a student here?"
"In a way, yes, but then again, in another way, not really."
"Tell him to show me his work."
"I will, but he's hard to pin down."

In the college refectory a week or so later a sociology lecturer walked over to me looking so grimly defiant that I feared I had offended her. She placed a slim folder with a bright tartan cover on the table beside my plate and said, "Read these poems. I typed them but they're written by Luke Aiblins, a truly remarkable student of mine."
"I hear he's a genius."
"He is, but needs guidance. Can I make an appointment for him?"
We made an appointment. She said, "I think I can ensure that he keeps it though it won't be easy. He's very hard to pin down."
She left. I glanced through the poems and saw they were beautifully spaced and typed. The first was titled PROEM. I read it with interest, re-read it with astonishment and a third time with pleasure. I then knew it by heart.

Bone caged, blood clagged,
nerve netted here I sit,
bee in stone honeycomb
or beast in pit or flea in bin,
pinned down, penned in,
unable to die or fly or be
any one thing but me,
a hypochondriac heart
chilled by the spittle of toads that croak
on the moon's cryptic hemisphere.

But yet, loft-haunter, tunnel-groper,
interloper among men,
I am the Titan & my pen
wet with blue ink or black
alone can tell them what they thought
and think and give them back
the theme, scheme, dream whose head
they broke, & left for dead.

Crown, King, Divinity: all shall be mine
to take, twine, make into a masterpiece
of fine thread, strong line.
Yes, let me write my life
ten volumes in one book
of good and bad friends, women who will
and will not walk with me,
the warped, harmonious, happy, sick & dead.
While I have eyes to look, so let it be. Amen.

All his other poems were equally resounding. I was now keen to meet him and quite unable to imagine him.

He kept the appointment and was a dazzlingly beautiful boy of eighteen or nineteen. His brown eyes and head of neatly curling brown hair harmonised perfectly with brown sweater and faun slacks. Relaxation and eagerness don't usually blend but in him they did. He entered with the happy air of someone who has all the love he wants while looking forward to more; entered silently, sat down, folded his arms and leaned toward me with an enquiring tilt of the head and encouraging smile. Beauty in people makes me want to stare with my mouth open. In men it almost strikes me as indecent, yet I felt a pang of envy that I quelled by turning my chair a little so that I looked past, not at him. As I cleared my throat to make an opening remark Aiblins said, "Excuse the question: why don't you look straight at me?"
"I look straight at hardly anyone in case they think me rude. I suppose I'm afraid of most people but I'm not afraid of their writings. I like yours very much. You know

that the rhymes of words inside a line matter as much as rhymes at the end. You know that the rhythms of lines in a verse can vary. You enjoy playing with the sounds of words and you make them entertaining for the reader."

"Right," said Aiblins, smiling and nodding.

"You have also learned from some very abstruse poets, Donne and Hopkins. Am I correct?"

"Eh?" said Aiblins.

"Have you read John Donne and Gerald Manley Hopkins?"

"No. Wait a minute. Yes. I once dipped into them but my work is original. I hear it inside this."

Aiblins tapped the side of his head with a finger.

"Never mind, Leavis says inspiration is often unconscious reminiscence. Now, creative writing teachers usually, and wisely, urge young writers to use the plainest, commonest words because many of the profoundest and loveliest and funniest ideas have been put into plain words. *To be or not to be, that is the question. I wish I were where Helen lies. So you despise me, Mr Gigadibs.*"

"No," said Aiblins reassuringly.
"I was quoting Browning. Now these well-meaning instructors forget that the same great wordsmiths very often relax or ascend into sonorous complexities: *sharked up a list of lawless resolutes, and Eleälé to the asphaltic pool, each hung bell's Bow swung finds tongue to fling out broad its name,* (and here I flatter you) *a hypochondriac heart, chilled by the spittle of toads that croak on the moon's cryptic hemisphere.* That line of yours is absurdly pompous, grotesque, almost insane but!" (I started laughing) "It works! We are often depressed for reasons we don't understand but feel are caused by something huge, vague and distant, something . . ." (I paused on the verge of saying *weird*, an Ian Gentle word) ". . . something uncanny that might as well be on the moon."
Aiblins, who had looked puzzled for a moment, smiled then said "Right."
"But I want to point out that these are the first poems of a very young writer, someone who is (please excuse the simile) like a bird flapping its wings to attract attention before launching into the air. You know that because it is your only

theme. You should now —"

"Excuse me," said Aiblins quietly yet firmly. "Are these my poems?"

He lifted the folder from the desk, glanced inside then laid it back, shaking his head, smiling and saying, "Yes, my poems dressed in tartan. Women are incredible. What can you do with them? You were saying?"

"The theme of all your poems is the great poet you are going to be. It is a prologue to your life's work, a convincing prologue, but not enough."

"Why not?"

"Take the first poem, the best, and the first verse, also the best: *Bone caged, blood clagged, nerve netted* et cetera. You are describing a state of confinement and frustration everyone has sometimes felt, poets and housewives and schoolchildren and ditch diggers and college lecturers. Right?"

"Hm. Maybe," said Aiblins.

"Verse two. *Loft-haunter, tunnel-groper, interloper* et cetera. Here you state your feelings of being both above and below other people, being *an outsider* as we called ourselves in the sixties, so you're still talking for a lot of people, especially young ambitious ones. Right?"

"You're getting warm."

"Then comes *I am the Titan and my pen* et cetera. You now declare yourself a masterful figure like Prometheus, someone who will help humanity recover something fine that it has spoiled and lost: innocence perhaps, faith, hope, love — only God knows what. So you are not now speaking for most folk, you are describing what only very confident priests, politicians, prosperous idealists, teachers, artists and writers sometimes feel, while speaking mainly for Luke Aiblins."

Aiblins smiled and nodded.

"Now look at verse three! *Crown, King, Divinity, all shall be mine.* What do these three words with initial capitals mean?"

"You tell me. You are the grand panjandrum, the salaried professor, the professional critic. I'm just a humble poet. You tell me my meaning."

"I think they mean that you feel sublimely smug because of your verbal talent."

"Do you think all my poems convey that?"

"I'm afraid so."

"Even the love poems?"

"Did you write any? Name one."

"OUTING."

Opening the folder I said "Let's hear it!" and read aloud the following.

This sunken track through the rank weeds
of docken, nettle & convolvulus
does not belong to us: only to me
whose nostrils gladly drank the stink
of vegetable sweat,
whose ears sucked in
the sullen whimper of the gnat's wing,
who gladly felt the wet sting of
smirr upon the cheek.

So do not talk, say no word to me
but walk in stillness on a path of moss,
a slope of trees upon our right hand side
and on our right the cluck & flow
of a wide stream.
I do not know what you see here.
I do not want to know.

For if each tries to see those things
the other sees
our probing eyes will shatter
the brittle matter of the other's dream
so each of us will be
inside a toneless, tasteless, aimless world
of mediocrity.

Walk in my dream and I will walk in yours
but do not try to share our separate dreams.
Two dreams can touch, I think,
but there's an end
of dreaming if we try to make them blend
for this can only be when both of us lie bare
and I have felt the ripeness of your flesh.

When bodies mix
then even dreams can melt.

"A love poem?" I asked, smiling.
"Why not?"
"It doesn't give the faintest idea of the companion it addresses, not even her or his sex."
"Shakespeare's sonnets aren't exactly portraits either."
"True, but it's clear the people he addresses are fascinating, and that he loves them. You tell your companion to shut up so that you can enjoy some very dull scenery, though at the end you seem to anticipate . . ."
I hesitated.
"Getting into her knickers?" suggested Aiblins.
"That's one way of putting it."
"Low marks for the start and the later poems. What about the last?"

"I'm glad you reminded me!" I said, greatly relieved, "At first it's bathos didn't impress me but now I think it is your best piece of verse – truly objective – not self-vaunting at all. You emerge here at last from the shell of your ego. Yes yes yes, here it is —"

A SPELL AGAINST ENVY

Rascals whose energy made history
had splendid banquets, buildings,
songs of praise
they never made. Digestion, rot and fires
undid their solid things. The finest hymns
cannot outlive the language of their choirs.

Only the joy of making things anew
outlive the owners & the makers too –
those fabricators, songsters, cooks who give
web, honeycomb, nest, burrow, beaver dam,
house, clothing, story, music & tasty stew.

"Though lacking the gaiety Yeats thinks essential this is a highly successful Marxist version of his poem *Lapis Lazuli*, " I cried, laughing.

"Never read it."

"Never mind. Perhaps you strain the last two lines by squashing into them every kind of animal and human maker you can think of, but it's still a good piece of serio-comic light verse. But the other poems resemble the efforts of a runner jogging up and down at the starting line before the pistol is fired."

"Another simile," said Aiblins brightly. "What are you reading these days?"

"Henryson's *Fables.*"

"You enjoy that stuff?" said Aiblins, incredulously.

"Yes. When I concentrate I find it astonishingly good. I'm concentrating just now because I'm reviewing a new edition of them for *Cencrastus.*"

"Hallelujah! Keep concentrating. I'm sticking to Shakespeare. Have you read *The Two Gentlemen of Verona*?"

"No. I've never even seen it acted."

"You should. It's great. Some idiots think he wrote very little of it but —"

For fifteen or twenty minutes Aiblins talked about *The Two Gentlemen of Verona* until I had no desire to read or see that play, then he looked at what seemed a new expensive wristwatch, apologised for having to leave now, lifted the folder, went to the door and paused to say, "Mark Twain."

"Yes?"

"Have you read his *American Claimant*?"
"No."
"You should. And don't blame yourself too much for the things you've just said. A couple of them made sense. Think on! I'll contact you when I need you. Cheerio."

I was left feeling horribly confused. Was he a genius? Was I an idiot? His damned *Proem* kept repeating in my head when I would have preferred to remember McDiarmid's *The Watergaw* or Hardy's *After a Journey* or even Lear's *Dong With the Luminous Nose*. Did that mean it was better than these? Impossible. But why could I not forget it? He had said he would contact me. A few weeks after seeing him I approached his sociology lecturer. She was chatting with colleagues in the staff club.
"Pardon me," I said, "Can you tell me how Luke Aiblins —"
"I can tell you nothing about Luke Aiblins except that he is mad, stupid, nasty and has, thank God, left this place for good." She turned her back to me.

The college changed its creative writing teacher every two years, perhaps to avoid paying a pension contribution due to regular teachers. I found similar jobs elsewhere, then had a book of poems published, then another. With an American friend I visited Edinburgh Castle and saw that an attendant in one of the regimental museums was Ian Gentle. I asked if the job bored him. He shrugged and said, "Not more than teaching, or punching railway tickets, or nursing in a mental hospital, or canning peas, which I have also tried. It's like reincarnation. You don't need to die to become somebody else. Have you read Schopenhauer's *The World As Will and Idea?*"

I had not and asked if he ever saw Aiblins.

"Poor Luke," said Gentle, "I'd rather not say anything about poor Luke."

I left the castle with a weird feeling that Aiblins would soon appear again.

Yet was unprepared when the phone rang and a voice said, "Luke Aiblins contacting you as arranged. Remember?"

"I remember you but remember no arrangement. It's years since you said you'd contact me."

"I'm doing it. I have a job for you. You're at home?"

"Yes, but —"

"I'll be there in ten minutes."

He hung up on me and arrived in four.

He was no longer beautiful because his nose was thickened and flattened except at the tip, which bent sideways. He was also haggard, with long bedraggled hair, and wore a shabby duffel coat and carried a duffel bag, articles I had not seen since my own student days. His manner was still eager but more tense. I asked if he would like tea or coffee.

"No thanks," he said, settling into an armchair with the bag between his legs. "Let's get down to business. You are at last able to help me because you are the king."

"What do you mean?"

"Poet Laureate of Dundee!" he said, grinning.

"I was born there."

"Honorary Doctorate from Saint Andrews University!" he said, chuckling.

"I was a student there."

"Winner!" he said, almost inarticulate with laughter, "Winner of the Saltire Award and a colossal Arts Council bursary for *Antique Nebula! Antique Nebula!! Antique Nebula!!!*"

"Have you read it?"

"Enough of it to see that it's crap, rubbish, pretentious drivel, an astonishing victory of sound over sense. You won't mind me saying that because you're intelligent so must know it's crap. I bet you often have a quiet wee laugh to yourself about how you've fooled the critics. Ours is a comic opera wee country with several comic opera imitations of English establishments. They're even thinking of giving us our own comic opera parliament! Our old literary crazy gang, MacDiarmid, Goodsir, Garioch, Crichton Smith *et cetera* were also crap but they've died or are dying and leaving your clique on top. You are now the boss and godfather of Scotland's literary mafia and at last in a position to help a real poet."

From the duffel bag he removed and handed me a thin, grubby folder with a tartan cover. I looked into it then told him, "These are the poems your teacher typed twelve years ago."

"Of course. You said you liked them, so prove it. Get one of your posh London publisher pals to print them. Tell them you'll write an introduction. Of course you won't know what to say so I'll write the introduction. It will appear under your name so you'll get the credit of introducing a great seminal book that won't give you any bother at all."

"Mr Aiblins," I said, "since you invoke the past let me remind you that I praised these poems for heralding much better work. Where is it?"

"Have you learned *nothing* in the past twelve years?" he groaned, then with an air of immense patience said, "The voice in my head says there is no point in dictating more poems to me before the first lot are in print, so to get the later poetry we *both* want, you must first get *these* published. Send them to Faber or Bloodaxe with a strong letter of recommendation by registered post tomorrow. Phone regularly at weekly intervals and pester them till they've read it and offered a decent advance against royalties and a definite publication date. And remember to photocopy them before posting because then you can send single poems —"

I said, "Listen —"

"No! Last time we met I did the listening, now it's my turn to lay down the law. In the weeks before publication prepare for it by getting single poems published in *Stand, Areté, The London Review of Books,*

The Times Literary Supplement, *Chapman* and *Cencrastus* beside good reviews of the book itself by well-known poets rather than academics. I suggest for England, Ted Hughes and Craig Raine; for Ireland, Heaney and Paulin; for Scotland, Lochhead and Duffy; for former colonies, Les Murray, Walcott, Ben Okri and Atwood. We have only one problem. My wife won't let me into our house, the people I'm staying with are trying to push me out, so for a while I'll have no contact address. Fear not, I do not plan to camp on your doorstep. I'll call here once a week for your report on developments at an hour *you*, not me, will choose. Make it as late or early as you please. Well?"

I said, "Mr Aiblins I am not the godfather of a Scottish literary mafia. There is no such thing. No firm will publish a book, no editor commission a review of it or print a poem from it because I order them. It is also many years since I was employed to show an interest in other folks' writing. I am now a selfish old bastard who cares for nobody's writing but his own. Please go away and tell that to as many other writers as you can. But you appear to be in poor circumstances. I am not. By a coincidence I refuse to explain I have seventy pounds in notes upon me. Here, take them. Goodbye!"

"You condescending piss-pot!" he said, smiling as he took the money, "But buying my poems won't get rid of me. I know they'll be safe here because your only claim to fame, your only hope of a place in world literature depends on them. So why postpone that? Your *Antique Nebula* will be forgotten long before critics notice where you got the few good lines in it."

"Are you suggesting that I have plagiarised you?" I cried, horrified, "I deny it! I deny it!"

"You sound as if you believe that," he said, frowning thoughtfully. "Perhaps you're unconscious of it. Perhaps most plagiarism is unconscious reminiscence."

"I am staring hard at that brass-topped coffee table," I told him, "because it is tempting me to lift it as high as I can in order to smash it down on your idiotic skull. But instead I will phone for the police if you do not take your poems and get the hell out of here."

"Dearie me, dearie me," he said waggishly. "I seem to have annoyed the poor old fat bald wee man. He must still envy me.

I wonder why?"

He strolled with bag and folder to the front door, which I opened. On the doorstep he turned and said quietly, "One last word of advice. Publish these poems under your own name then try to live up to them. You'll fail, but the effort may make a real man of you, if not a real writer. And think of the fame you'll enjoy! I won't resent that because great poetry is more important than fame. Here, have it."

I closed the door on him. A moment later the folder, bent double, fell in through the letter box. My self respect felt as if it had been squeezed between the heavy rollers of a mangle. His poems were so strongly associated with this feeling that I could not bear to pick them up. Opening a cupboard holding gas meters I kicked them inside and locked them in. I so dreaded hearing from him again that I fixed an answering machine to my telephone and never took a call direct, but he never called again.

Time passed away. So did the Berlin Wall and the Russian Empire. In *The Times Literary Supplement* I read reviews of abstruse books by the former Marxist student who liked classical opera and now had a medical practice in Stuttgart. I discovered that the little Chinese girl who once visited me was now an award-winning feminist poet who wrote popular, very gruesome crime thrillers under a pseudonym. I read her works closely for signs of my influence and detected none at all.

One day I heard a friendly, eager voice say, "Hullo, how are you doing? What are you reading these days?"

I stopped and after a moment recognised poor Aiblins. He was completely bald with many bruises on his head and face and many unhealed cuts between them. He wore jeans, a leather jacket and shambled in a way I had not seen before, but his battered features had amazingly recovered the happily relaxed expression I had first envied.

"What happened to your face, Luke?"

"Oh, I had an argument in a pub with a man who glassed me so it became a police matter. I mean the police took me in and gave me a doing before turning me out. But it was all just usual reality, it doesnae matter. Have you read *The American*

Claimant yet?"
"Not yet. Can I buy you a drink?"
I said this because we were in a street very far from where we might be seen by people I know.

After two unsuccessful attempts we found a pub that would serve him and sat with pints in a quiet corner. I admitted I had not yet read *Two Gentlemen of Verona* and steered the talk away from literature by asking if he ever saw his wife nowadays.
"Neither her nor my son. In fact she kicked me out before he was born because she hated the name I was going to give him – a lovely name it was too, a perfect poem in itself: *Tristram Pilgrim Aiblins.*"
He announced the name with great enthusiasm then repeated it slowly as if separately enjoying each syllable, then he asked if I knew what it meant.
"*Tristram* means *sadly born,*" I said, "I'm not surprised the mother didn't want her boy called that."
"You've forgotten what Aiblins means. That makes a difference."
"What does Aiblins mean?"
"Look it up, wordsmith," he said, laughing. "Consult a Lallans dictionary,

you antique Scottish nebula."
"But how did you know a son was coming before he got born?"
He tapped his brow saying, "I heard it in here."
I asked if his inner voice ever gave him poetry nowadays. He said, "I think it's trying to. Sometimes a good line gets through but never a whole couplet or verse because the government is jamming me."
"The government? How?"
"It keeps sending other voices into my head, loud ones that accuse me of terrible things I've never done, never even imagined doing. Why? Why should the government spend money on elaborate broadcasting equipment just to torture me with false accusations only I can hear? It makes no sense. It's a total waste of taxpayers' money."
He did not say this angrily or miserably but with a kind of puzzled amusement. I said, "Some people in high places must think you very dangerous."
"Yes, but why?"
"Tell me a line your inner voice has given you recently."
He pressed a finger to the side of his brow and after a while said, "*Since breathing is my life, to stop I dare not dare.*"

"I like that line. Any more?"
"Er . . . *Great vessels sink, while piss-pots stay afloat.*"
"Better and better. Do you still think I'm a piss-pot?"
He grinned apologetically and murmured, "If the cap fits . . . Oh, here's another coming through: *To die, to me, today, is like returning home from a war.*"
"That's the best line of all. You're still a poet, Luke, in a fragmentary way."
"The government must want to keep me fragmentary. Has your inspiration ever been broken up by outside broadcasting?"
"No."
On his discoloured, distorted face appeared a smile of pure childish happiness mingled with sly mischief.
"Your work isn't good enough to frighten them," he murmured and gave my shoulder a consoling pat.
"True. I must leave now."

I gave him money that he tranquilly accepted. I hurried away in a state very near panic. By pretending to share his world view I had almost been convinced by it. I was glad to learn later that the *dare not dare* line came from the introduction to John

Lennon's *In His Own Write*, that the sunk ship and floating piss-pots were from a translation of a Gaelic proverb in one of McDiarmid's most rambling monologues. I haven't found the source of the third, which may be a genuine Aiblins invention. But I am afraid to re-examine the verses in the creased folder in my lobby cupboard, afraid to show them to people who might judge them differently. It might emerge that I have driven a great poet insane by suppressing his earliest works.

For the same reason I fear
to destroy them.

PROPERTY

WHEN LONDON WAS ADVERTISED as the world's fashion capital – when The Beatles seemed the nation's greatest export – when a Conservative prime minister with a Scottish name said, probably truthfully, that the British people had never been so prosperous, two such people went for a weekend camping holiday in the Highlands.

They were building workers of seventeen and eighteen who lived with their parents in the town of Dumbarton. On Friday night after work they packed the panniers of their motorbikes, rode up the Vale of Leven, took the shore road by Loch Lomond to Tarbert, turned west to the head of Loch Long then zoomed over

The Rest-and-Be-Thankful. As darkness fell they passed through the Highland's only neat little eighteenth-century town and began looking for a camping place. There was a sea loch to their left, hedged fields to the right, and after a mile or two they saw a side road with a wide grassy verge. Here they stopped, spread a groundsheet, erected a tent and put the motorbikes inside. This left enough room to lay down sleeping bags with the panniers for pillows. Then they tied the tent flaps shut, walked back to the town and spent a pleasant evening in the bar of a small hotel.

There are many tales of Scottish country pubs serving drink after the legal closing time. This was one such pub. The boys, cheerfully drunk, left it after midnight and returned to the tent through a mild but sobering rain shower. They sobered completely on finding the tent flaps wide open and nothing but the groundsheet inside. They discussed returning to the town and phoning the police but gloomily decided that a Highland policeman might be hard to rouse at that hour, especially if the rousers were urban youths smelling of drink. They agreed to do nothing before daylight and spent a miserable night huddled in their leather clothes back to back on the groundsheet.

At eight in the morning they were themselves roused by a man wearing well-cut tweed clothes and accompanied by a policeman. To the boys this man seemed very tall and fresh-faced, perhaps because they felt tired and dirty. He said, "You have insolently camped upon my land without asking my permission. What have you to say for yourselves?"
The elder boy said they didn't know that the roadside was not public, also that their motorbikes and other things had been stolen.
"Not stolen. Impounded," said the man, "I had them removed last night to the police station. You can thank your lucky stars that I was kind enough to leave you the tent. So now dismantle it, collect your chattels from the station and clear out. I do not object, as a rule, to visitors who behave properly and drop no litter. I regard this – " he indicated the tent – "as a form of litter. I have a friend, a very brave soldier who had similar trouble with a family of

people like you. Well, he discovered their address, went with a friend to the municipal housing scheme where they lived and pitched a tent of his own in the middle of their back garden. They didn't like that one little tiny bit. Quite annoyed about it they were as a matter of fact."

The man turned a little and looked steadily toward the loch, mountains, glens, rivers, moors and islands that he regarded (with the support of the police) as his back garden.

15 FEBRUARY 2003

MY PARENTS TAUGHT ME that getting attention by unconventional actions (they called it "showing off") was bad manners. By pleasing teachers, broadcasters, publishers and others in authority I have become a noted author and Professor of Glasgow University. Why should I walk with many others through the centre of Glasgow, complaining about a government that lets me vote for or against it at least once every five years? I am not driven by *esprit de corps*, take no pleasure in feeling part of a crowd travelling in the same direction. Most goodness, truth and beauty has been achieved by people like Jesus, Galileo and Van Gogh who were out of step with crowds of people. Soldiers marching in unison appal me as much as a line of high-kicking chorus girls appals ardent feminists. I only take part in political demonstrations when I feel it wickeder to stay away: a state first experienced in 1956.

I was then a student who, twice a week on his way to Art School, called at a clinic for injections to reduce allergies causing asthma. As I bared my arm for the needle one morning a nurse treating me said, "What do you think of this war?"
"What war?"
"The war with Egypt. We invaded it two days ago – we and the French and the Israelis."
"But . . . but what's the BBC saying about it?"
"The BBC hasn't said anything about it yet, but it's in all the morning papers."

This war is called the *Suez* war because Britain and France were fighting to get back control of the Suez canal which Egypt had nationalised the year before. Israel was fighting because Egypt had barred it from what had been an international waterway. Like the USA's war with Vietnam the Suez war was never openly declared. The British public and Parliament only heard of it on the third day when the government could no longer keep it an official secret. I hurried out of the clinic, excited by my certainty that public opinion would drive that government (a Tory one) from office in a week. I was naïve.

Though fellow students at the Art School were excited by the news not all were horrified by what I considered a lawless action, even when the BBC broke silence and announced the RAF was bombing Alexandria, chief seaport of a nation without an air force. A friend who I thought was socialist said cheerfully, "The old lion is wagging its tail again!"
Like most of the popular press he thought the war a revival of imperial health. I heard an anti-war rally was being held in Glasgow University Union, rushed there and found it a rally against the USSR invasion of Hungary, which was happening at the same time. Like everybody else there I too decided to forget the bombed Egyptians in my sympathy for the invaded Hungarians.

The Suez invasion killed 22 Britons,

10 French, about 200 Israelis and 921 Egyptians, yet Britain and its allies lost that war because the United Nations, the Vatican and the United States condemned it – also the British Parliamentary Labour Party. Yes, I voted Labour then because Labour (I believed) had created a welfare state and abolished government by stock exchange (unlike the USA) and was part of a nation providing a democratic alternative to single party dictatorship (unlike the Soviet Union). I was grateful to the Labour Party for my healthcare, my further education and for condemning the Suez War.

I was happier still when a large majority of local Labour parties voted for Britain to abandon nuclear weapons: another good example we were giving to the world. But the Labour Party leaders rejected the majority opinion of the ordinary members who had voted them into Westminster. On this matter Labour MPs sided steadily with the Tories. By 1965 the London parliament's ability to turn local Socialists into British Tories had moved me to vote for Scottish home rule, which we are far from having achieved in 2003.

Britain now has a government to the right of Mrs Thatcher's, for hers spent more on social welfare than Mr Blair's. So did John Major's. Blair supports President Bush who has decided to break the Geneva Conventions by not just invading a country that cannot invade ours, but also occupying it in order to change the government. Bush declares that Iraq has acquired genocidal weapons of the kind the USA, Russia, Britain, France, India, China, Israel also possess, which makes us terribly nervous. To paraphrase Miss Jean Brodie, "Do not do as I do, little nation, do as I say." Can anyone doubt that if the USA and Britain backed a United Nations plan to inspect and catalogue the dangerous weapons of every nation it would be implemented? Of course every nation would have to include the USA and Britain and Israel. Saddam possesses evil weapons because Britain and the USA sold them to him and the means of making them. In the 1980s he was our ally and used them to exterminate many innocent Kurdish people, but now, in 2003, Kurds are fleeing *into* Iraq to escape from the government of our ally, Turkey. Certainly he arrests people on suspicion and imprisons them without trial or legal advice, but since 11 September 2001 George Bush's government also does that.

That Iraq contains more oil than any other single nation – that the USA would fall apart without cheap petrol – is one reason for this war. Another must be a widespread desire in the USA to see some brownish turbaned Islamic folk suffer for what happened on 11 September 2001. An internationally orchestrated police investigation would not look sufficiently dramatic on television. The invasion of Afghanistan was not enough. It killed more civilians than those who died in the World Trade Centre, but bigger explosions, larger troop movements are needed by a President whose cuts in social welfare funding have damaged his popularity without curing a depressed US economy. And of course USA businesses and military leaders want total control of the world's oil wells.

A third of the British troops taking part in this war and occupation will be Scottish, though Scotland has a tenth of Britain's population. The Scots were hiring themselves out to foreign armies many centuries before our union with England. I regret that tradition so I am going to Glasgow Green, and thanks for a sunny day, God.

Arriving with wife and lawyer friend I am amazed by the *many* crowds spreading from the triumphal arch before Glasgow High Court to the People's Palace in the east and Clyde on the south. All demonstrations contain weirdly dressed people who delight the hearts of antagonistic reporters, but here they are so outnumbered as to be invisible. Yet this multitude is splendidly un-uniform, though I hear the women of the Euridice Socialist Choir singing a peace song and some vendors of the Scottish Socialist Party newspaper. There are people of every age, from toddlers in prams pushed by parents to elderly men like me. Some carry doves made of white polystyrene, there are many printed placards saying '*Make War on Want, Not Iraq*', '*Not In My Name, Mr Blair*' '*No Blood for Oil*' and asking for Palestinian liberation. Some hand-made ones are less serious. A nice woman upholds '*I Trust No Bush But My*

Own', a stout bearded gent shows the *'Dumfries Ageing Hippies Against the War'* logo. Two boys of ten or eleven walk carefully side by side wearing a single sandwich board made of card with slogans written in fibre-tip pen. They seem to have no adult presiding with them.

There seem no adults presiding over anyone, so we join the crowd at its thickest beside Greendyke Street where the procession should start, edging in as far as possible and looking around for guidance. It is provided, unexpectedly, by the police. They form a barrier between the crowd and the street and let us through in numbers that can start walking ten abreast, thus filling the width of the road without flooding pavements on each side.

We await our turn in this good-natured, very patient crowd. I can see none of the friends I had arranged to meet on the Green, see several others in my line of business: novelists Bernard MacLaverty, A.L. Kennedy, the poet Aonghas MacNeachail, several teachers and lecturers. Some senior citizens carry a banner saying THE TAYSIDE PENSIONERS' FORUM. My lawyer friend tells me Blair proposes to abolish old age pensions because workers' contributions are now too small to pay for them, I suppose because of inflation. This steadily reduces the wages of the poorest paid while used as a reason for taxing the wealthy less, thus letting them invest more in private businesses of global extent. So New Labour may undo the main achievement of Lloyd George's Liberal government in 1908! We talk about the arms industry: how the 1930s depression only ended when Britain and the USA prepared for war, how both nations have been preparing for war or fighting it ever since, how the making and export of weapons is now Britain's main industry and trade. Then I remember that the Principal of my University, Professor Sir Graham Davies, is chairman of the Universities Superannuation Scheme, a pension scheme of which many British academics are members and which (a handbill tells me) has £60 million invested in British Arms Enterprise. Some students a month ago were threatened with expulsion from Glasgow University for protesting against such investments. Should I not have supported them? But I have eaten, drunk and conversed with Principal Professor Sir Graham Davies, a cheerful, friendly soul who has been very supportive of my university department. It would embarrass me to criticise him publicly. Yes, at heart I am an arselicker.

I often get letters nowadays from people keen to discuss or discover views of Scottish *identity,* as if more than five million folk could possibly have a single identity. But if asked what chiefly characterises my nation I will repeat what I wrote in 1982: arselicking. We disguise it with surfaces of course: surfaces of generous, open-handed manliness; surfaces of dour, practical integrity: surfaces of maudlin, drunken defiance: surfaces of quiet, respectable decency. The chorus of a Scottish national anthem proposed by a Dundonian poet comes to mind —

Hermless, hermless, naebody cares for me.
I gang tae the libray, I tac oot a book
And then I gang hame for ma tea

— as I usually do. There have been many eminent Scots with strong independent minds but now the most eminent are the worst arselickers. Scots Labour MP's lick Tony Blair's bum. Tony Blair licks the bum of the US President. Any US President. It's a British Prime Ministerial tradition.

At last the police are letting us through and, roughly ten abreast, we process down Greendyke Street then up the Saltmarket to Glasgow Cross. Occasionally those around us burst into wild cheering, seemingly inspired by folk waving encouragement from upper tenement windows. Our stream divides neatly to pass the gawky clock tower of the Tollbooth, all that remains of Glasgow's seventeenth-century Town Hall, magistrates' court and city jail.

In John Prebble's book about the Glencoe massacre I read that two British officers were imprisoned there in 1692. They had opened their sealed orders before reaching Glencoe village, and found themselves ordered to put men, women and children to the sword. They broke their swords and told their commander at Fort William that no decent officer should obey such an order. So they were sent south by ship and jailed for a while in this Glasgow Tollbooth. Prebble says there is no other record of them so they may have escaped further punishment. I would love to see a big plaque on that tower commemorating these two brave soldiers. Scotland's castles, cathedrals, public parks, city centres contain many many war memorials, some of the most elaborate commemorating a few officers and men who died in Africa and Asia while killing hundreds fighting on their own soil without the advantage of gunpowder. Are these two officers the only British soldiers to disobey a dishonourable order? Then I remember hearing that in the Gulf War authorised by the last President Bush, four British officers resigned their commissions in protest against dropping those cluster bombs which "mince up everything that lives within a three-mile strip" onto Iraqi ground forces, though most UK and US airmen queued up enthusiastically to airstrike such folk, who could not strike back. One bomber said they looked like swarms of cockroaches.

From the helicopter that sometimes passes above us we too probably resemble cockroaches as we ascend the High Street, turn left down Ingram Street, turn left then right again. Our biggest roar goes up as the Civic Chambers come in sight. Why are there no Glasgow Town Councillors waving from those upper windows? My wife reminds me they are on holiday because this is Saturday. Why are there none in our procession? (I am delighted to learn later there is one, at least.) Approaching George Square on the St Vincent Street side we can now see a silhouette of the procession crossing the summit of Blythswood Hill a quarter mile ahead.

Coming abreast of an Irish pub we call in for a refreshment, emerging half an hour later to join the procession behind the banner of Unison, the local government employees' union. A small brass band is playing a melancholy Scots ditty and I am astonished to find myself on the brink of tears. This sentiment owes nothing to a recent sup of lager. Our huge movement is composed of Scottish workers, tradespeople, professional people who identify with them – all people I feel at home with. These folk will suffer most if our businessmen take the advice of an expert in Scottish Enterprise, formerly known as The Scottish Development Agency. He has advised Scottish businesses to have their goods made by workers in Eastern Europe or Asia.

We arrive in a desert of car parks covering the site of the former Princess Dock, a vast basin surrounded by huge cranes where giant ships unloaded cargoes and took them aboard during the Suez War when Glasgow was a great international port and centre of manufacture. The huge car parks are more crowded with multitudes than Glasgow Green. Beyond them I see some big arched metallic structures that seem to have slid out of each other, a building locally nicknamed The Armadillo. I realise for the first time that this Armadillo is the Glasgow conference centre. A line of yellow-jacketed police is looped protectively around it. From the height of an open-topped double decker bus near the river someone is making a speech, but loud speakers are banned so few phrases are audible. Some storms of applause are heard and we hope the Prime Minister hears them and sees how many we are. We later learn, however, that —

(A) Tony Blair did not speak to the Scottish Trade Union conference in the afternoon, as scheduled, but changed it to ten in the morning so he could leave

the district, and perhaps Glasgow, before we left the Green, and
(B) The speaker aboard the bus was Glasgow's Lord Provost, or the leader of the Scottish Socialist Party Tommy Sheridan, or a spokesman for the Church of Scotland, or for Scotland's Asiatic communities, or for the CND, because all made speeches from there.

After half an hour we come away, moving against the flood of people still approaching from the City Centre, for the procession has been longer than its three mile route. The ruler of Britain will learn nothing from this peaceful rally, or those in New York, Sydney and most major European capitals. Are the commanders of armies in great and small, rich and poor nations right to think that only destructive violence can defeat destructive violence? No. Within the last forty years, tyrants ruling by force of arms and torture in Greece, Spain, Portugal, South Africa, Russia gave way to kinder, more democratic rulers without invasion and warfare. What that Jewish extremist, Jesus, preached from a small hill near Jerusalem, was not idiotic.

WELLBEING

I SAW A PLAIN STREWN WITH marble rocks, the smallest higher than a man, the largest as big as a cathedral. They were pieces of a statue that had once stood taller than Ben Nevis. Groups of little people moved with horse-drawn wagons among these rocks. They were searching for a piece recognisably human yet small enough to carry away – the lobe of an ear or tip of a toe. Each group wanted to put such a fragment where they could love and pray to it, as it would prove there had once been power, beauty and unity that the world no longer contained. A group found a rock pierced by a beautifully smooth oval arch, part of a nostril. As they lifted it into their cart other groups combined to attack and rob them. This happened to all who found a good fragment, so none was ever carried away and love and prayer were impossible. I opened my eyes because my Japanese host was asking a question.

"In the second chapter of book ten you say *till all the seas gang dry, my dear*. My useful dictionary defines *gang* as a band of ruffians or criminals, a number of labourers working together. None of these definitions seems to fit."
I said that *gang* was also a Scottish transitive and intransitive verb meaning *go* and these words were a quotation from Robert Burns's greatest love song. My host murmured politely, "I believe Robert Burns's poetry is still sung in parts of North America."
I nodded. I was happy.

We were in the Smooth Grove, which had been the Central Station Hotel in days when Glasgow was joined to other places by railway. I felt the luxury of a good meal in my stomach, good wine on my palate, clean socks, underwear and shirt against my skin. They had been worth waiting for. Foreign translators, journalists and writers of dissertations always buy me new clothes before standing me a lunch – posh restaurants won't let me in without new clothes after I've slept a few weeks in ones the last foreigner bought me. Foreigners contact me through my bank. Ordinary pubs and all-night cafés accept me since I can pay for drink and food and can sleep in short snatches sitting upright.

I was not always dependent on foreigners for a smart appearance. I used to have several friends with homes and visited each of them once a fortnight. They gave me food and a bed for the night and put my clothes through a machine. Modern machines not only wash, dry and iron, they remove stains, mend holes, replace lost buttons and re-dye faded fabric to look like new. Or am I dreaming that? If I am dreaming such a machine it is certainly possible because, as William Blake said, nothing exists which was not first dreamed. Most of these friends steadily disappeared but were not, I think, stabbed or burned. People with homes still usually die of diseases or a silly accident.

My one remaining friend is now my first wife who pretends to be my daughter. I don't know why. I visited her a month ago. After

enjoying a plate of her excellent soup I asked how Mavis was getting on in London. She stared and said, "I am Mavis. Cathy is dead – died twelve years ago, shortly after I came home."
"Nonsense Cathy!" I said. "You can't be Mavis because Mavis quarrelled with you and she was right to quarrel with you because you were not kind to her, though I was too tactful to say so at the time."

My host in the Smooth Grove was as ancient as I am and still used a notebook. Looking up from it he said, "I hear there is now no middle class in Scotland and England. Is that true?"
I told him it was not true: the middle class are those who used to be called working class – they have jobs but no investments, and their only pensions are state pensions.
"But middle class implies a lower class. Who are they?"
I explained that thieves, swindlers, rapists, drug dealers and murderers are our lower class nowadays, many of them registered with the police. They have a place in society because without them police, lawyers, judges, jailers and journalists would be unemployed, and the profits of

drug companies would slump.
"So in Britain everyone has a place in the social fabric?"
"Everyone but the homeless," I answered, trying to remember why I feel perfectly secure though I am one of these.

My host started writing again and to avoid disturbing thoughts I dreamed of a future state in which human police had disappeared because the rich no longer needed them. The rich never left their luxurious, well-defended homes except when visiting each other in vehicles moving at the speed of light. Each home was protected by a metallic creature the size of a kitten and resembling a cockroach. It hid under chairs and sideboards and was programmed to kill intruders. I was a low-class criminal who broke into the apartments of a rich young sexy woman, cunningly reprogrammed her police creature to serve me, then enjoyed a number of sexual acts which appeared to be drawn in a highly coloured, very entertaining strip cartoon of a kind which became popular in France at the end of the twentieth century and in Britain at the start of the next, though many British people then were still able to read. We had a very entertaining country in those days. I had been teaching abroad since the late seventies and every time I returned the changes struck me as so interesting that I wrote about them.

Yes, one year publishers sold my stories to a newspaper cartoon supplement for so much that I stopped teaching and brought my second wife home to Glasgow. She was from Los Angeles or Chicago, I think, and believed that life for prosperous people was the same anywhere, and indeed Britain was now very like America. The police only patrolled the streets of prosperous ghettos where householders had bought crime insurance. The police observed other communities through public surveillance cameras and had power to swoop in and uplift anyone on suspicion, but they mainly lifted unregistered politicians and folk who owed money to drug dealers. When people fell down in the street it was no longer etiquette to help them up or summon an ambulance. We hurried past knowing that next day they would probably be gone. I had a lovely home in those days. I lost it in a wave of inflation which suddenly made life *astonishingly* interesting. My wife returned to the USA. I stayed out of curiosity though

British publishing had stopped. Not even newspapers were produced. Industries with a use for wood and rag pulp bought the remaining libraries. Some books are still used to give public houses an old-fashioned look. Boys' adventure stories from the 1910s predominate.

My host said, "Toward the end of your eleventh book you mention *no concurrency of bone*. What do you mean by that?"

All foreigners ask that question. I can now answer it without thinking. While doing so I closed my eyes and enjoyed walking on a grassy hilltop beside a tall, slender, beautiful young woman I had loved when I was fifty. Even in this dream I knew our love was in the past, that my virility was dead and that no beautiful woman would ever love me again. I told her this. She grew angry and called me selfish because I was only dreaming of her to cheer myself up. This was obviously true so I forgot her by staring at a hill on the far side of a valley, a Scottish hill soaring to Alpine heights with all the buildings I have ever known in rows between strips of woodland, heather and rocky cliffs. On the crest of the mountain I saw the red sandstone gable of the tenement where I was born in 1934, at the bottom I recognised the grey clock tower of the Smooth Grove where I was dining and dreaming. The scene delighted me by its blend of civilisation and wilderness, past and present, by the ease with which the eye grasped so much rich intricacy. Suddenly the colour drained from it. The heather turned grey, the trees leafless, but I still felt perfectly safe and remembered why.

Though still telling my host about the massacre of Glencoe and Ezekiel's valley of dry bones I remembered the death of Mr Anderson, a former radio announcer with whom I once shared a kind of cave, a very safe secret little hidey-hole, we thought, in a shrubbery of Kelvingrove Park. In those days I had not learned to sleep in small snatches while sitting upright so I slept by drinking half a bottle of methylated spirits. One morning I woke to find my companion had been stabbed to death and scalped. I did not know why I had been spared until several weeks or months or years later. Perhaps it was yesterday. I'm sure I did not dream it.

I stood on the canal towpath enjoying a glorious gold, green and lavender sunset when I was tripped and knocked down. I lay flat on my back surrounded by children of seven, eight or nine. Their sex was not obvious. All wore black jeans and leather jackets. All had skulls and crossbones painted or tattooed on top of heads that were bald except for a finger length of small pigtails all round. One poured petrol over my trousers, the rest waved bats, cutting implements, firelighters and discussed which part of me to bruise, cut or set fire to first.

"We are the death squad of the Maryhill Cleansing Brigade," explained the leader who was perhaps eleven or twelve. "We are licensed terrorists with a sacred mission to save the British economy through a course of geriatric disposal. Too many old gerries are depressing the economy these days. If you can't afford to get rejuvenated, grampa, you should have the decency to top yourself before becoming a burden to the state."

I told him I wasn't a burden to the state, wasn't even a beggar, that money was paid into my bank account by foreign publishers and was enough to feed me

though not enough to rent a room.
"You pathetic, hairy old driveller!" shouted the leader, goading himself or herself into a fury. "You're an eyesore! The visual equivalent of a force-nine-gale fart! You will die in hideous agony as a warning to others."
I was alarmed but excited. To die must be an awfully big adventure. Then a small fat person with glasses said, "Wait a bit, Jimsy, I think he's famous."
They consulted a folded sheet with a lot of faces and names printed on it. The fat person, who could read names, asked if I was Mr Thingumajig, which I am. They helped me up, dusted me down, shook my hand very solemnly one at a time, said they would remember me next time we met, said they would gladly kill any old friend I wanted rid off, advised me not to go near a naked flame before my trousers were dry, hoped I had no hard feelings. Honestly, I had none at all. My gratitude and love for these children was so great that I wept real tears. The leader got me to autograph the printed sheet. It was pleasant to meet a young Scot who still valued my signature. The sun had not yet set when they left me. I watched the gloaming fade, warm in the

knowledge that I had a privileged place in modern Britain. Not only the children liked me but their bosses in the Cleansing Company or Social Security Trust or Education Industry or whoever had a use for children nowadays.

Yes, somebody up there likes me even though once I detested the bastards up there, the agents and consultants, money farmers and middle men, parliamentary quango-mongers, local and international monopolists. My books were attacks on these people but caused no hard feelings, and now my books are only read in nations that lost World War Two.

My host spoke on a politely insistent note. “I suggest you visit my country. Your royalties there will easily rent a private apartment with housekeeper and health care. We are no longer a military nation. We revere old people, which is why they live longer among us than anywhere else.”

I said I was happy where I was. He shut his notebook and bowed saying, “You are a true master. You have subdued your wishes to your surroundings.”

This angered me but I did not show it. There are better ways of living than being happy but they require strength and sanity. The poor and weak are as incapable of sanity as the rich and powerful. In this country sanity would drive the weak to suicide and make the rich distinctly uncomfortable. We are better without it.

END NOTES AND CRITIC FUEL

DEDICATION: Agnes Owens is the most unfairly neglected of all living Scottish authors. I do not know why. It is not because she worked for years as a house cleaner in a district of high unemployment, since working class origins and experience are often put to an author's credit. Nor has she been ostracised by other Scottish writers. Liz Lochhead first read one of her best stories – *Arabella* – in the 1970s, when she met Mrs Owens at a writing group in the Vale of Leven. Liz introduced her work to several other Scottish writers who admire it. In 1984 James Kelman introduced to Polygon Press *Gentlemen of the West,* her first novel, which became a Penguin paperback. Two collections of her stories have since been published and four short but perfect novels, the last (*Bad Attitudes*) by Bloomsbury in July 2003. Though not widely reviewed all her reviews have been highly favourable, yet she is never remembered when awards are handed out. Perhaps she is ignored by publicists because they cannot believe a creative intelligence can thrive long in a council housing estate.

BIG POCKETS WITH BUTTONED FLAPS first appeared in *New Writing 9* published by Vintage and the British Council in 2000.

NO BLUEBEARD The naming of this

man's wives by number is taken from *Eventide*, a novel Roger Glass, one of my students in Glasgow University Creative Writing Programme, began writing in 2002.

JOB'S SKIN GAME was conceived as a monologue when eczema recurred to me after an abeyance of nearly forty years. I connected the monologue with ideas in the Book of Job when Lu Kemp, a director of Scottish BBC Radio, commissioned a modern story from me based upon that Book. This story, in a shorter version, was broadcast by BBC Scotland in January 2003 and printed in *Prospect*, April 2003.

SINKINGS. The two hideous experiences in this story befell my friend, Peter Gilmour.

AIBLINS is an old Scots word meaning 'perhaps'. The tale is partly based on my experiences as a writer employed by Glasgow University between 1977 and 1979, and non-connected with my experiences as a professor (with J. Kelman and T. Leonard) between 2001 and 2003. Ian Gentle is a real person; Luke Aiblins a composite of several, but chiefly of myself. The *Proem* and *Outing* poems were part of a sequence I wrote in my late teens and luckily failed, despite many efforts, to get published, though my friend Robert Kitts recorded many of them for his television documentary *Under The Helmet* networked by the BBC in 1964. A shorter version of *Aiblins* was published by the magazine *Prospect* on 17 April 2003.

PROPERTY is based on what happened in Argyllshire to the sons of my friend Bernadette Logie.

15 FEBRUARY 2003 is based on a *Herald* article published on 17 February 2003.

WELLBEING was the last chapter of a political pamphlet, *Why Scots Should Rule Scotland,* Canongate, Edinburgh 1997.

CREATIVE WRITING was the title of a 13th story which I discarded as too facetious. It contained three jokes I will inflict upon you here —

FICTION EXERCISE

When three years old I saw my parents killed in a road accident and decided never again to love anything else that can bleed.

Use the preceding sentence to start a short story or novel.

BOOK REVIEW EXERCISE

Queneau's *Le Chiendant* explores the existential consequences of radical changes of epistemological perspective.

Without loss of intelligibility rewrite the preceding sentence using the word paradigm.

LOGIC EXERCISE

Query: Which is the odd man out?

Tiny Tim
Little Nell
Wee Willie Winky
Moby Dick
(Remember that one of them is female)

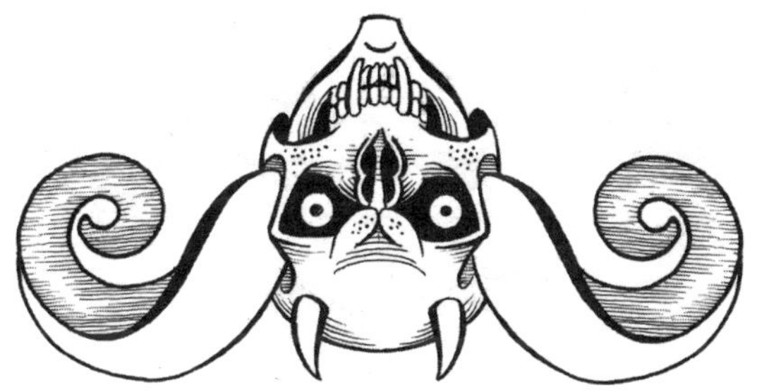

Answer: All four are fictional mammals but only Wee Willie Winky is immortalized in rhyme.

GOODBYE